Copyright © 2025 by Carolynne Wilson

Disclaimer

This is a work of fiction set in an alternate history. While this book may reference real people, including public figures, their portrayal is entirely fictional and does not represent actual events, beliefs, or actions. Any resemblance to real individuals beyond the context of well-known public information is purely coincidental.

Names, characters, places, and incidents are either the product of the author's imagination or are used fictitiously. Any resemblance to actual persons, living or dead, or to real events is purely coincidental or to support the fictitious storyline. The inclusion of real names does not imply any factual basis or connection to actual individuals. The views and actions expressed by the characters are solely those of the fictional personas created by the author and should not be attributed to any real person.

This book is a speculative narrative and is not intended to depict or suggest real-world events, past or present. The views, statements, and actions of all characters—including those with real names—are products of the author's imagination and should not be interpreted as factual claims or endorsements.

Contact
thelegacy@sectorconnect.org

SECOND EDITION

Chapter 1
A Paradox of Love and Legacy

Ruth Rossiter had always been a walking contradiction. The irony of her existence was impossible to ignore. Her mother's family had fought tooth and nail against the anti-aging drug Gnia-itra, insisting that if it couldn't benefit the masses, it shouldn't benefit anyone. And yet, here she was—a product of the very exclusivity they despised. Without Gnia-itra, she wouldn't exist. Talk about a complicated family legacy.

Sperm and egg donation? That was old news by 2056. But using the frozen eggs of a long-dead wife to bring a child into the world twenty-one years after her passing? That was a whole new level of eerie devotion. Ruth's father, Stanley Rossiter, had stepped boldly into that strange frontier, a man fuelled by grief, love, and a desperation to find what was lost.

He never remarried after Janey—Ruth's mother—died in 2035. How could he? Janey wasn't just his great love; she was the argument of his life. Their debates were the stuff of legend—passionate, endless, and always circling the same battlefield: the pursuit of immortality. Stanley, obsessed with defying death, willingly sold pieces of his soul (and a considerable fortune) for access to Gnia-itra. Janey, on the other hand, would have rather died—literally—than betray her principles. She saw the drug as a weapon of power, creating a divide between the elite and common people.

Her convictions ran deep, woven from generations of justice seekers. Even before Janey's mother—Joan Ruth Bader Singsburg—was stripped of her right to practice law and forced off the bench, the Singsburgs had dedicated themselves to the relentless pursuit of fairness and equality. Janey carried that torch fiercely, unwilling to compromise, not even for the man she loved. Not even to stay with him a little longer.

And yet, she left behind one small loophole. Her eggs. A quiet act of love wrapped in defiance, an unspoken acknowledgment that maybe—just maybe—there were forces even stronger than principle. And so Ruth was born, an improbable fusion of her father's relentless determination and her mother's unshakable ethics, delivered by science, nurtured by devotion, and shadowed by contradiction.

It wasn't the kind of birth story you shared casually, but after learning the truth Ruth had embrace the absurdity of it. If nothing else, she was proof that contradiction didn't just exist—it thrived.

Janey had been built for battle long before she met Stanley. As a teenager in the 1970s, she cut her teeth volunteering at Legal Aid, starting with coffee and filing before moving on to real advocacy work for at-risk youth. It was an era of seismic shifts—Vietnam, Roe v. Wade, the rise of Earth Day. She watched Nixon fall in disgrace and Shirley Chisholm rise with audacity. She witnessed America fracture, heal, and fracture again, and with every moment, she became more certain of her calling: justice was not a privilege. It was a right. A fight. A duty.

Stanley, by contrast, came from a world she called "privilege on steroids." Private schools, inherited wealth, doors flung open on command. It wasn't that he lacked ambition—he simply never had to prove himself. Where Janey clawed her way into Harvard on merit and scholarship, Stanley strolled in on a gilded path paved by his father's chequebook. Even the library bore their name, a conveniently timed "philanthropic donation" ensuring his admission.

And yet, despite—or perhaps because of—their differences, they fell in love. Deeply, madly, irreversibly. They were fire and ice, argument and affection, locked in a passionate, endless debate about everything. Especially Gnia-itra. To Stanley, it was salvation. To Janey, it was a betrayal of everything she stood for.

Even in death, Janey refused to yield. Her final wishes were absolute—no experimental resurrections, no desperate grasp at what was lost. And though defiance ran through Stanley's veins, he honoured her will.

But love, real love, doesn't just disappear.

Long ago, they had frozen her eggs, a quiet promise to a future that never arrived. There was always another mission, another breakthrough—always something more important than pausing to build a family. And then, time stole her away.

Stanley had nearly forgotten. Nearly.

Then, twenty years after she was gone, the fertility clinic called. The past roared back like a tempest, grief crashing into him with the force of a life unfinished. But Stanley was a pragmatist, a man who understood that loss could be transformed, that endings could birth new beginnings.

So, with a heart heavy yet resolute, he made the only choice he could. He gave Janey a future—through their child.

In her later years, Ruth would wonder what her mother would have thought of her. A daughter conceived through a technology Janey would have abhorred, yet also born of love so deep it defied time. But Ruth had long since learned to live with the contradiction. After all, she wasn't just an accident of science or a stubborn man's refusal to say goodbye.

She was something more—a living testament to the impossible coexistence of love and principle, of justice and defiance. And if that wasn't legacy, what was.

Chapter 2
The Unspoken Truth:
Unravelling the Past

As a child, Ruth lived a life that seemed plucked from the pages of a fairy tale. Each morning, she awoke to the symphony of singing birds drifting through the sprawling gardens of the Rossiter estate. Her days were a harmonious blend of piano lessons, horseback riding, and afternoons immersed in the grand library—a sanctuary of leather-bound books where she would lose herself in stories far beyond her years. A small army of attentive staff catered to her every whim, and each night concluded with enchanting tales spun by her grandmother, Evelyn, whom Ruth lovingly called "Mama." For Ruth, life was idyllic, serene, and unchanging. She never questioned it—why would she?

Yet, beneath the veneer of her storybook existence, a faint longing stirred within her, a restless yearning she couldn't name. Evelyn's love, though genuine, was like the delicate porcelain teacups she cherished—exquisite but fragile, never spilling over.

Everything changed on her ninth birthday in 2062.

The day was nothing short of magical, a testament to the grandeur of the Rossiter name. White tents adorned the garden, a string quartet serenaded the guests, and a cake stood taller than Ruth herself. Family members whose names she scarcely remembered surrounded her, their smiles as polished as the gifts wrapped in shimmering paper. Yet, amidst the opulence, Ruth felt a peculiar loneliness, as if she were adrift in a sea of faces.

Then, a man approached her, his smile warm but tinged with sadness.

"Hello, Ruth. My name is Raymond. I'm your cousin," he said gently.

Ruth tilted her head, her innocent curiosity unguarded. "You seem awfully old to be a cousin."

Raymond chuckled softly. "I am. Your mother, Janey, was my aunt."

A puzzled look crossed Ruth's face. "My mother's name isn't Janey. It's Evelyn."

Raymond hesitated, his expression softening. "No, Ruth. Evelyn is your grandmother. Your mother was Janey Singsburg Rossiter."

Ruth's brow furrowed. "Is she here?"

Raymond's smile faded. "No, sweetheart. Your mother passed away a long time ago. But there are other family members who would love to meet you."

Before Ruth could respond, her father, Stanley, appeared, his voice sharp. "What are you doing here, Raymond?"

Raymond's gaze remained steady. "It's time, Stanley. She deserves to know."

Stanley's face crumpled, emotion welling in his eyes. Sensing the tension, Ruth asked softly, "Father, are you alright?"

Stanley knelt beside her, his voice breaking. "I'm alright, my darling. Just…sad. But I'll be fine once Raymond and I chat inside."

He stood, placing a protective hand on Ruth's shoulder before leading Raymond toward the house. Evelyn intercepted them, her tone icy.

"Stanley, I trust you're showing this person out?"

Stanley's jaw tightened. "No, Mother. It's time. Ruth needs to know, and the Singsburgs deserve to love her, just as we do."

Evelyn's composure faltered. "But…but—"

"Enough, Mother," Stanley said firmly. "It's time, and I'll sort this out with Raymond. Please, leave us be."

In the library, the air was heavy with unspoken truths. Raymond's voice broke the silence. "You're right, Stanley. It's time. You should have sought our family's consent for what you did. But you didn't, and now we're here. Ruth deserves the truth."

Stanley's shoulders sagged under the weight of his remorse. "I know. I should have spoken to your family, but I was so consumed by grief. Losing Janey left a hole in my heart, and when they approached me about her eggs…it felt like a glimmer of hope, a chance to bring back a piece of her without breaking my promise. I was afraid your family would deny me that."

Raymond's expression softened, the harsh edges of his reproach giving way to understanding. "What's done is done. But now, we must face this together. Ruth deserves to know who her mother was, and she deserves the love of her entire family."

Stanley nodded, his voice resolute. "You're right. It's time she knows everything."

Chapter 3
Unveiling the Past:
A Journey into Family and Secrets

Ruth's world didn't vanish that day in 2062. It expanded.

The Rossiters had built a universe where her every whim was met with a snap of the fingers. Need a playmate? One appeared. Craving pancakes? A feast materialised. It was magical. It was manufactured.

The Singsburgs were something else entirely.

Raymond took Ruth to meet them, a trip that felt both exhilarating and terrifying. Their home, nestled in a lush green haven, was smaller than Ruth's bedroom wing.

Her first introduction? Conney, a girl her age, who greeted her with an unexpected bellow: "WELCOME, AUNTY RUTH!"

Ruth blinked. "I am... an aunt?"

Conney nodded solemnly. "Yes. And I will now show you everything."

Raymond barely managed to contain his laughter as the two girls engaged in what could only be described as the most courteous shouting match in history, as Conney dragged Ruth through a whirlwind tour of the house.

Ruth was a little nervous about who she would meet, but she decided to focus on Conney. To her surprise, Conney was very talkative.

"What's it like to be born in a lab?" was Conney's first question.

Astonished, Ruth replied, "Don't you remember?"

Conney giggled "No silly! I was born in my mummy's tummy"

"Oh, of course," Ruth muttered, perplexed by the idea of growing inside another human being, but decided to hold her questions until she could understand more. As they toured the house, Ruth's curiosity grew.

It was strange for Ruth to be inside such a small house, and it was difficult for her to imagine that more than one person lived there. It was the size of her wing at home. The décor was eclectic, with framed photographs, art, and handmade crafts spread throughout. There was only one place to eat meals: the kitchen. The large wooden table at the centre appeared to be a gathering place for family meetings and community discussions, as several people were sitting around it when Conney and Ruth walked in.

They all rose and approached Ruth, giving her hugs and saying their names. It was all very strange, although not that unpleasant. Although she wasn't used to hugs, she quite liked them.

Conney's mother was Alex, Raymond's sister, and Simone was his other sibling. These three people were Ruth's cousins, the nephew and nieces of her mother, Janey. They all knew her mother, and during their hugs, they all said variations of the same thing: "Your mother was brilliant and so kind."

Their father, Janey's brother, had passed away some years ago. The lady who didn't rise to greet Ruth was Valda, their mother and Janey's sister-in-law. Despite remaining seated, she greeted Ruth warmly, saying, "Welcome to my home, Ruth. We've all wanted to meet you for a very long time."

"I'm sorry I didn't come earlier; I didn't know you were my family. If I had, I would have come sooner," Ruth responded.

"Of course, dear, we understand. We are very excited to get to know you and tell you all about your mother," said Valda

"Oh, how wonderful," Ruth exclaimed. "I'm eager to learn about my mother and get to know you all."

A computer and numerous books were on the table. Simone asked, "Have you ever seen a picture of your mother?"

"No, is there one," Ruth asked hesitantly

"Yes, we have many," Valda replied.

"We've gathered them for you here," Simone added. "We also have digital copies, but thought you'd like to see the printed ones first."

"Oh yes, please, I'd love to," Ruth said. The only physical photos she had ever seen were on her grandmother's bookshelf, and she wasn't allowed to touch them.

When she opened the first album, Ruth was struck by a photo that looked just like her. "We thought you'd like to see your mother at your age. I am amazed by how closely you resemble her," Simone said.

The photos unveiled a new world to Ruth, each image a doorway to her mother's life. She eagerly flipped through two of the five albums prepared for her, questions multiplying in her mind.

"I'd like to study these photos and ask you more questions later. Can I take them home?" Ruth asked.

"Of course," said Valda. "We made them for you."

The rest of the day was filled with stories of her mother's intelligence, kindness, and community spirit. Ruth's mind buzzed with questions but refrained from interrupting the tales.

Finally, she couldn't hold back, "Do you remember when she died?" Ruth asked.

"Yes, we do. It was a very sad time," Simone said.

"What happened, and why did it take 21 years before I was born?" Ruth asked.

"You need to talk to your father about that. He will explain it to you," Simone replied.

Before Ruth could delve further, the conversation shifted to when she could visit again. Conney eagerly asked, "Can you please come to my house next time? There's so much I want to show you."

"I'll need to ask my father, but I'll beg him to say yes," Ruth said, her excitement undimmed, despite knowing her grandmother's reluctance about today's visit.

Chapter 4
Echoes of Revolution:
A Soundtrack of Love and Change

In 1973, Janey and her friends were utterly besotted with Pink Floyd's *The Dark Side of the Moon*. This wasn't just an album—it was practically their life soundtrack. No matter where Janey went—whether it was a rowdy party, a carefree car ride, or those notoriously awkward study sessions—those iconic melodies were like a cosmic mantra on repeat. Little did she know, this album was also about to ignite her grand love story.

Enter Stanley, a fellow aficionado of the psychedelic masterpiece, who had been orbiting Janey's universe for quite some time. They'd seen each other in class, sharing shy glances like two satellites on a collision course, but neither had mustered the courage to speak. That all changed one fateful night at a friend's house party. Picture this: dimmed living room lights, a sea of beanbags and lava lamps, and a haze of thick smoke that could've rivalled London's fog. Ironically, Janey and Stanley were the only two not stoned. They were clumsily twirling on the makeshift dance floor, propelled solely by youthful exuberance and the magnetic pull of the music.

As destiny (or gravity) would have it, they bumped into each other. Janey, startled yet intrigued, gazed into Stanley's wide eyes. The moment stretched endlessly like one of David Gilmour's legendary guitar solos.

"Don't you just love this Pink Floyd?" Janey asked, her voice tinged with wonder.

Stanley paused as if savouring the gravity of her question. "You can't beat it," he replied, his tone as deliberate as the album's ticking clocks. Then, in perfect harmony, they both added, "I love it."

The universe must have been in on the joke because they burst into laughter, their voices blending seamlessly with the dreamy soundtrack. From that moment on, *The Dark Side of the Moon* wasn't just an album—it was their anthem. Its intricate themes of time, madness, and mortality mirrored their profound conversations, while its pioneering sounds reflected the sparks of their budding romance.

Over time, the album became their secret weapon. Whenever their arguments spiralled out of control, one would cue *Time* or *Us and*

Them. The music acted like a magical balm, dissolving their tension and pulling them back into each other's orbit.

In the end, Pink Floyd united Janey and Stanley and bestowed upon them a love story as timeless as the album itself.

Meanwhile, Ruth, who knew the album well from her father's constant replay sessions in his study, was finally beginning to understand the magic through Raymond's stories. She wished her father had shared these tales with her himself.

As Raymond's car pulled up to the driveway where her father stood waiting on her return from her first visit from the Singsburgs, Ruth hesitated to step out. Sensing her unease, Raymond asked, "Are you okay?"

Ruth took a moment, then looked up at him and said, "Promise me you'll come back, Raymond, and that I can visit you all again."

"Of course, Ruth. This is just the beginning. We're so excited for you to become an active member of our family." Ruth didn't quite grasp what that entailed at the time.

"Thank you for coming to find me, Raymond. It's made me very happy."

"You're very welcome. Is there anything you'd like me to say to your father?"

"No, I have lots of questions, but I'll ask him myself." With that, Ruth opened the car door and leapt out.

Raymond also got out but didn't approach Stanley. Instead, he simply said, "Thank you, Stanley. We had a wonderful day, and I'll be in touch to set up a regular schedule."

Stanley didn't speak; he merely nodded. Raymond slowly drove around the fountain in the middle of the driveway and departed.

"Did you have a lovely day?" Stanley asked.

"Yes, but I'm very mad at you," Ruth replied candidly.

"I know, darling. I hope one day you'll be able to forgive me," he said, his voice tinged with regret.

"Me too. I have lots of questions, but first, I need to find a special place for these albums they gave me," she said.

"Can I see them?" he inquired.

"Not yet. I want to study them first. Then, I want a meeting with you in your study, where

I'll have lots of questions for you," she declared in her most mature tone.

"Alright. If you go to your room, I'll arrange for a snack to be sent up," Stanley responded, his heart a mix of pride and sadness.

As she walked off, she yelled, "Thank you, Father."

Ruth poured over each photograph, her fingers tracing the edges as if she could uncover the thoughts and emotions coursing through her mother at the time. The pictures spanned decades, forming a timeline Stanley would recognise when Ruth finally confronted him in his study.

Janey, always at the heart of the action, is pictured holding up signs in many photos, sometimes among friends and sometimes in determined solitude. Stanley took some of the pictures, capturing the essence of their era. They speak of a history painted with passion and conviction.

In the 1970s, the slogans shouted from the placards were: "Make Love, Not War," "ERA Now!" "My Body, My Choice," and "Save the Earth."

The Eighties roared with calls for change: "No Nukes!" "Silence = Death," "Free Nelson Mandela," "Stop Reaganomics."

The Nineties demanded attention with cries of "No Blood for Oil," "Out of the Closet and Into the Streets," "Think Globally, Act Locally," and "Save the Rainforest."

At the turn of the millennium, we heard: "Not in My Name," "We are the 99%," "The Planet is Burning," and "Yes, We Can!"

As the decade progressed, the signs evolved, reflecting the continuing struggles and hopes: "Hands Up, Don't Shoot," "Time's Up! " "There Is No Planet B," "Never Again."

By the 2020s, the calls for justice and equality seemed even louder: "Black Lives Matter," "My Body, My Choice," "Stop Asian Hate," "We Stand with Ukraine," "Act Now or Swim Later," "Trans Rights Are Human Rights."

Each photograph told a story, a chapter in Janey's life, fuelled by the fiery spirit of activism and a quest for justice. Ruth felt a profound connection to her mother through these images as if she were journeying alongside her through the decades of change and resistance.

She knew that when the time came for her appointment in Stanley's study, these photos would be her guide, allowing Stanley to give the context and depth she needed to understand her mother's heart and mind. Although she didn't understand many of the protest signs, in her heart and from the stories she had now been told, she knew that they represented causes her mother had passion for and, collectively, expressed her empathy for others and desire for a better life.

Chapter 5
A Delicate Balance:
Loyalty, Secrets, and New Alliances

2065 Ruth's world continued to blossom with new experiences, vibrant connections, and delightful conversations. Though it was evident her grandmother, Evelyn, wasn't exactly thrilled about the direction their dinner table discussions had taken. Since that life-altering conversation between Ruth and her father, the pair explore topics that had once been off-limits in his study. Ruth had bravely confronted Stanley about why he'd kept mum about her mother and the baffling 21-year delay before he finally decided to use her mother's stored eggs to have her.

Eager to unlock the mystery of her parents' love story, Ruth had asked Stanley to start from the beginning. His eyes sparkled as he recounted the early days, his voice laced with fondness. He laughed about their silly squabbles, but what stood out most was his unshakable respect for her mother's strength and steadfast moral compass. "I swear, she'd pick fights with me just for fun," he grins. "She knew I'd back her, even if I didn't always get where she was coming from."

They had been so engrossed in their hectic lives that they decided to freeze her eggs early to expand their family when the time was right. "But when we were finally ready, your mother thought she was too old," Stanley said, a tear gleaming in his eye. "She didn't think bringing a child into the world at her age was fair."

Ruth frowned in confusion. "But how could she be too old? You're still young, and you're older than she was."

Stanley sighed. "That's something I need to explain. It's one of the biggest disagreements your mother and I had. There's this vitamin tablet—a drug, really—that I hope you'll start taking when you're the right age. It prevents aging, and I've been taking it for a long time. Your mother, though, was against it."

"But why?" Ruth asked, bewildered. "If it keeps you healthy?"

Stanley's expression darkened. "She called it the genocide drug. Only the elite got access to it—an exclusive few. She saw it as a way of condemning everyone else to the dustbin while those at the top grew more powerful. To her, it was a crime against humanity."

When piecing together what she had learned about her mother's family and comparing it to how she was raised, Ruth asked, "Is that the difference between mother's family, the Singsburg's, and ours?"

Stanley nodded solemnly. "Yes, to some extent. My father was incredibly wealthy and a close friend to the President. We're considered part of the Calaberras, a class above the rest."

"So, mother never took the drug?" Ruth asked.

"No," Stanley said, voice tinged with sadness. "I tried to convince her. I said if she wanted to fight for equality, to ensure everyone had access to it, she'd have to live long enough to make that happen. But she wouldn't listen. We argued endlessly, but I couldn't change her mind."

"Oh, dad," Ruth said softly, giving Stanley hope that she was beginning to understand as she never called him dad. "I'm sad she didn't take the drug. I want her to be here now, but I'm proud of her for sticking to what she believed."

"I know, honey," Stanley said, his voice thick with emotion. "I've never stopped missing her. When the agency contacted me about her stored eggs, it brought me back to life."

"Well, if you didn't use the eggs, I wouldn't be here," Ruth said with maturity beyond her years. "And I'm grateful for that. But I'll need to think about whether I'll take this drug."

Stanley nodded, relief flickering in his eyes. "We'll talk about it when you're ready. But for now, how about we look through some of your mother's photo albums?"

They spent hours reminiscing, Stanley spinning stories behind each picture while Ruth mentally noted every detail to write down later. This was the start of many joyful conversations, once forbidden in their home but now blooming like fresh flowers in a garden.

As Ruth delved deeper into her new life with the Singsburgs, she couldn't help but marvel at how different it was from her old world. Rossiters had been obsessed with appearances, status, and material wealth, but the Singsburgs cared about *life*—about the planet, equality, fairness... and, inevitably, politics. Ruth had never been exposed to this level of activism before, but now, she was swept up in it.

Ruth found herself in a whirlwind of new experiences, things she had only read about in books. Then there was Conney, who had redefined what true friendship meant to Ruth. Conney was always there, checking in, sharing secrets, and offering her a glimpse into a life of meaningful connection.

The Singsburgs weren't just a family; they were a *movement*. They all had a role to play. Donald Crumpt Sr. was nearing the end of his life, and this was a hot topic of conversation for the Singsburgs and a catalyst for new Alliance efforts. Gnia-Itra drug could prevent aging, but it couldn't reverse it. Crumpt had started taking the drug late in life, and now he was reaching the end of his days. This was an opportunity to rise against this system that favoured only a few.

It was a lot for Ruth to take in, but she was starting to see the world through new eyes. And she was interested!

Then came the conversation that would mark a turning point in Ruth's life—one that would forever alter the course of her involvement with the Singsburgs and her future. The resistance they formally called the Alliance had been unsuccessful in influencing change, so in June 2066, just after Crumpt Sr. passed away and the Presidency passed to Donald

Crumpt Jr., Raymond sat Stanley down for a serious chat.

"Stanley," Raymond began, his voice low but urgently charged, "Although you would never betray your family, I know you always supported Janey. You've seen the direction things are going with the Calaberras and the rest of the world, right?"

Stanley had to think for a few minutes before answering. He knew that when Stanley set up this meeting, he would want something from him, but this wasn't the conversation he was expecting.

"I've always loved my family," he began cautiously, "but I get what Janey was fighting for."

"Well, Stanley, we don't want you or Ruth to do anything that would harm your family, but the Alliance does have an ask of you," said Raymond cautiously.

"I don't want Ruth involved in anything dangerous, so you can forget any ask of her," said Stanley.

Raymond was unruffled. "It's not dangerous. We're asking for *insight*. We need Ruth to build relationships with the Calaberra children and, if you can, with their parents. We've been trying to break through for years but need a different approach."

Stanley was perplexed. "Why us? We don't have anything in common with those people."

"Because you do, you are Calaberra," he said, "You could be the bridge we need."

"That sounds like a lot of work, you know I'm not very social, and Ruth has been pretty isolated from those people," said Stanley.

"I know," said Raymond, "but there may be two benefits for Ruth. Those people might convince her to start taking Gnia-Itra, which I know you want, and she would broaden her network to help her in the future."

"What is the benefit to the Alliance," asked Stanley.

Raymond's expression grew more serious. "We need information. You and Ruth would be in the perfect position to feed us intel on the Calaberras, which would help us shape a strategy to influence their thinking."

Stanley's stomach churned. "You want us to spy on them?"

Raymond was blunt. "Yes. In a way, yes."

Although Stanley knew what Ruth's response would be, he still said, "I will need to discuss this with Ruth,"

"Yes, of course, but please do not discuss it with anyone else; we need to keep this very close to our chests," said Raymond.

"I can guarantee you I will not be discussing this with anyone else," he said, looking at Raymond as if to ask, "Do you think I'm stupid?"

Seeing Stanley staring into the distance, Raymond waited for him to return to the discussion, "If we move forward, I will be doing this for Janey."

Raymond nodded.

Stanley pondered on how to approach Ruth. He knew she would automatically say yes, but he wanted her to understand the gravity of the decision. A slip-up and it could all fall apart with terrible consequences.

That evening, Stanley casually asked Ruth to join him in his study after dinner, making sure not to draw any attention from his ever-watchful mother. Once they were comfortably seated opposite each other in his plush lounge chairs, he began.

"Ruth, how have you found spending time over the past few years with the Singsburgs?" he asked.

Worried that he might feel abandoned, Ruth replied, "I love spending time with them, Dad. I've learned so much. But I want you to know I still love you."

Stanley smiled at her use of "Dad," a rare but welcome term. "I know you do, honey. But there's something important I need to talk to you about."

Her expression grew serious. "What is it?"

"Do you know about the Alliance?" he asked.

She looked a little shocked. "Yes, I wasn't sure if you knew about it."

"Although I might not have agreed with it, I always supported your mother. We never had any secrets. But I have not been involved since her death," he responded.

"Oh, yes, I know some things, but I know how important it is to keep it to myself," she replied.

"Well, I have had a discussion with Raymond, and it is a very serious matter that I wish to share with you," he said. "I want you to think carefully about what I am going to ask you, as it could have major consequences if things go wrong," he said very seriously.

"What is it, Dad?" she asked.

"Raymond has asked if we will help the Alliance," he responded.

"Yes, of course!" Ruth nearly jumped out of her seat with excitement.

"No, Ruth, I want you to listen to me first, then we can make the decision together," he said, followed by, "They want us to make friends with the Calaberras and to build relationships with them. They have a long-term goal of hoping to influence them in the future to think differently about humanity and help with a peaceful transition to a new world."

Ruth blinked, taken aback. "Spies?" she asked with a smirk.

"Well, we would be walking a tightrope. We don't want anyone to get hurt, but we would need to feed information back to the Alliance that would help them develop plans to influence the Calaberras," he said. "We would need to start going to parties and lunches, and you will need to change schools."

Ruth's desire to be of value to the Alliance outweighed any disappointment she might feel about changing schools. "Oh, Dad, I can do it; we can both do it for Mother," she said, trying to respond in a mature voice.

"Okay, I have a few ground rules which we can go over with Raymond. I'll set up a time we can meet and discuss," he said. "Oh, and one important thing—you cannot discuss this with anyone, including Grandma Evelyn."

Ruth nodded, eager but understanding the weight of the decision. "I'm ready."

And thus, Ruth's next chapter began one that would force her to walk a fine line between loyalty, love, and the pursuit of justice.

Chapter 6
Undercover Beginnings:
The Art of Infiltration

The year 2066 was well underway when Stanley was ready to start devising the undercover plan for himself and Ruth. He wasn't exactly a James Bond type—more of an "I'll observe quietly from the sidelines" kind of guy—but he knew that to succeed, they needed precision, patience, and a touch of subtlety. Their mission? To infiltrate the upper echelons of the Calaberras, build connections, and gather intel—all without raising any suspicions. It was going to require finesse and a lot of acting natural. Something Stanley was... less than confident in.

Stanley had consistently declined invitations to Calaberra's events or engaged at a deeper level to honour Janey's memory, and he had never held his own events. But now, he was about to plunge headfirst into a world of glitzy parties and shallow small talk.

Despite his reservations about this espionage venture, Stanley was thrilled by its ability to bring him and his daughter closer. Ruth impressed him with her maturity and intelligence, reminding him of Janey.

The first step? Moving Ruth out of her beloved Montessori school, which had nurtured her individual genius, and into the high-powered, elite institution known as *Haleberry Academy*. The school was practically a breeding ground for the kind of families they needed to connect with. It was also closer to their home, which made the logistics of their new life easier to pull off. Stanley worried that Ruth might change her mind about transitioning to a new school, but he needn't have worried.

She had already devised a cover story: She wanted to finish middle school at the Academy because it would give her better prospects for college and her future.

So, they used this as a starting point to build the plan for their new lives.

The plan included weekly meetings with Raymond at their home. They figured that if they established this routine now, it wouldn't seem suspicious later when they were deep into their 'spying' activities.

As Stanley and Ruth aimed to build relationships, Stanley took Ruth to school on her first day. As they were leaving, Evelyn came into the hall and asked, "Why are you taking Ruth to school? Surely Henry (their butler) could take her."

Stanley stammered a bit at first. "I...I... want to meet her Principal to discuss the types of activities the school offers."

Finding this strange, Evelyn asked, "Why would you want to do that?"

"I think it's time I started taking a more active role in the world around us," he responded without hesitation this time.

Shrugging, Evelyn said, "Well, I'm glad to hear that at last."

As Stanley parked the car and exchanged a quick, knowing look with Ruth, a silent bond passed between them. It was their little secret—one they shared in the quiet intimacy of their shared mission.

Out of the car, Ruth went her way, and Stanley headed towards the office.

Ruth's first day at Haleberry was a whirlwind of new faces, new dynamics, and a whole new set of rules. And while Stanley had left her to her own devices, he had already set up a meeting with the principal, Ms. Ellis. The plan was simple: appear supportive, concerned, and eager to connect with the other parents. It was important to plant the right seeds now so that when the time came, he could use those connections to his advantage.

Ms. Ellis, a sharp woman who had probably never had a bad hair day, greeted Stanley at the front desk and led him straight to her office. She was impressive, tall with dark hair, wearing glasses that seemed to say, "I know things you don't." Stanley did his best to act normal.

"Thank you for taking the time to meet with me," he said, trying not to sound like he was about to reveal he was a secret agent.

"Of course, Mr. Rossiter," Ms. Ellis replied smoothly. "We always enjoy meeting our new parents."

"I know how busy you are, so I'll get straight to the point," he said confidently. "I'm a little worried Ruth might find it difficult to adjust to moving from a Montessori school to a more traditional educational program."

Ms. Ellis immediately bristled as though he'd insulted her entire life's work. "Mr. Rossiter, I wouldn't describe our school as 'traditional'. We're highly adaptable to each student's needs and are constantly evolving."

"Oh, of course, I didn't mean it to come out that way. I just want to help Ruth settle in," said Stanley.

"Naturally, no offence taken. There are many avenues of support available to both you and Ruth. We have a parents' forum each fortnight where parents can discuss any ideas they may have about improving any aspect of our school," said Ms Ellis.

"Wonderful. I embarrassingly admit that I hadn't focused on Ruth's education as I should have, so I am very eager to change that and would appreciate attending such an event," said Stanley.

"You would be very welcome, Mr. Rossiter," she said.

"Call me Stanley, please," he said a bit timidly.

Meanwhile, Ruth had spent a lot of time talking to Conney. They were excited about a new technology that allowed you to send a message just by thinking once a chip was implanted. It was called Airplay, but they weren't sure how private their conversations were, so they kept them light. Only Stanley, Raymond, Conney, and Ruth knew about Ruth and Stanley's involvement with the Alliance. So when Conney and Ruth met in person, they couldn't stop talking about it, brainstorming ways to make Ruth's transition to Haleberry and her new role as a spy as smooth as possible.

Raymond and Stanley tried to advise them, but Ruth and Conney would roll their eyes. The conversations usually went something like this:

Stanley's advice: "If you want to make friends, Ruth, you should act super confident, pretend you know everything."

Raymond's response: "No, that isn't it. You need to be discreet. Just slowly take your time and, in the lunchroom, sit with different girls."

Conney's retort: "That might be how you did it in your day, but you have no idea what it's like to be a teenager today. Leave that bit to us."

Ruth and Conney knew popularity was a game of image, and to win, you needed to be a mix of cool, mysterious and slightly approachable. While learning how to play this at Haleberry, it was best for Ruth to keep a relatively low profile at first, but not so low that she was overlooked.

They knew there would be the usual groups, such as the "popular girls," the "goths," and the "nerds." None of them could be dismissed as they might be the most influential, but you may never know unless you dig deep.

For Ruth, that meant playing it cool with the "popular girls," waiting until they invited her into their circle. As for the goths, well, she'd need to know their music, their books, and their whole vibe. It wasn't just about blending in—it was about understanding them on a deeper level.

In the end, it was a game of observation and adaptation. Ruth learned from the people she met and passed the information on to Conney, who dug deeper into the backgrounds of their subcultures. They were a team—a sub-Alliance unit, just the two of them.

And so began Ruth and Stanley's undercover journey, navigating the treacherous waters of high society and teenage dynamics in the name of a cause greater than themselves.

Chapter 7
The New Kid's Game: Navigating Haleberry's Social Labyrinth

Ruth realised that imagining herself as the new kid at Haleberry and being the new kid at Haleberry were two very different things. She'd always been welcomed with open arms in new situations. But Haleberry wasn't just another school but a battlefield of cliques and unspoken hierarchies. And being *the new kid* felt much less glamorous than she'd imagined.

Even her assigned "best friend" for the day, Alicia, seemed to think the job was beneath her.

The plan was simple: Alicia would meet Ruth on the fifth step of the library stairs an hour before her first class to show her around. Easy, right? Except it wasn't. Forty-five minutes later, Ruth was still sitting on the fifth step.

"Did I mess up the meeting spot?" she wondered aloud, scanning the area for any sign of her no-show guide.

A sharp voice cut through her thoughts. "Hey! You Ruth?"

Ruth turned to see a girl standing at the bottom of the stairs, hands on hips, exuding an energy that screamed, *"I am not here to please you."*

"Yes, that's me," Ruth replied, making her way down to meet the person she assumed was Alicia.

"Hi," she said in her most upbeat voice. "You must be Alicia."

The girl snorted. "Not even close. Alicia bailed and sent me instead. I'm Arabella."

"Oh." Ruth forced a polite smile. "Well, nice to meet you, Arabella."

Arabella's grin was equal parts charming and devious. "Pro tip: don't tell Ms. Ellis that Alicia ditched. She'll have a meltdown."

Ruth shrugged. "Fine by me. We're good as long as you can show me to my first class." Thanks to a meticulous map-reading session with Conney, she didn't mention that she already knew the layout.

"Sure, but don't expect a VIP tour," Arabella said, already walking. "I've got better things to do, and I'm only here because Alicia made me.

And just so we're clear—this doesn't make us friends."

Ruth decided "Okay" was the safest response. There was no point pushing her luck too soon. Ruth had picked this place to meet as it would take time to walk to her first class, giving her a chance to pick Alicia's brain. Clearly, that wasn't going to happen.

However, as they walked, Ruth realised Arabella wasn't as tight-lipped as she pretended to be. "So, here's the deal," Arabella said, tossing her hair. "Ms. Ellis always picks Alicia to be the 'newbie whisperer.' But Alicia's got better things to do, like running this school. So, she sent one of us to see if the new kid's worth her time."

Ruth raised an eyebrow. "So, I'm being evaluated?"

"Pretty much," Arabella said with a shrug. "But hey, maybe you'll pass the test. Or not. No pressure."

Ruth chuckled. "Good to know."

And just like that, her Haleberry adventure was underway—a crash course in social politics, clandestine tests, and high-stakes survival. Game on.

Ruth hadn't considered how different the school's approach to learning would be. She was used to being encouraged to explore subjects at her own pace and follow her interests. This was very different; students moved through the same material at the same pace, which was mind-numbingly dull and surprisingly easy for Ruth.

Ruth quickly identified Alicia from her very first class. The teachers loved her; she was practically their co-pilot.

"Alicia read the passage on page five."

"Alicia, what do you think of Ryan's interpretation?"

"Alicia, can you take over the class while I step out?"

It was like watching a teacher's pet in high definition. Meanwhile, Ruth was busy taking mental notes for Conney.

Then there were *The Unnoticeable*—the quiet kids in the back row who seemed to blend into the walls. Ruth might've missed them if she hadn't been extra observant. They never spoke, even during group work, and the teachers barely acknowledged their existence. It was eerie but intriguing.

Ruth noticed patterns everywhere. Alicia's influence was far-reaching, and her "minions" were easy to spot—uniformly dressed with matching jewelled necklaces. Ruth wasn't in all of Alicia's classes, but one of her proxies always seemed to pop up.

Ruth was pleased she had something to report to Conney on her first day. Although it was nothing groundbreaking for the Alliance, at least she had observations she could share.

Although Conney and Ruth's schools were close in proximity, the students rarely mixed. However, to support Ruth, they agreed to meet at a Haleberry student hangout spot three times a week—half homework, half spy work. Conney had advised Ruth to keep their connection vague in case anyone asked. "Say your dad makes you hang out with your cousin. Throw me under the bus if you need to," Conney said seriously.

By the time Ruth arrived home, dinner was ready, so she and Stanley didn't have a chance to debrief before they saw each other at the dinner table. Despite their bubbling excitement about sharing updates, they managed to play it cool.

Evelyn surprised them by saying, "I'm so glad you two are spending so much time together, and Stanley, I am so happy you have decided to meet new people."

"Thank you, mother. I need to be more proactive if I'm to be a good role model for Ruth," he said.

"Good. Ruth needs to expand her circle. She is spending too much time with the Singsburgs. She needs to spend time with her own people," responded Evelyn.

Months ago, Ruth and Stanley would've bristled at that. Now, they exchanged a subtle glance and nodded in unison.

"How was your first day at Haleberry," her grandmother asked.

"Interesting, Alicia Sherlock was supposed to show me around, but she couldn't make it, so a girl called Arabella was very helpful," Ruth said.

"The Sherlocks are a wonderful family, Stanley. You went to school with Prudence Sherlock, do you remember?" Evelyn asked.

"She was a little younger than me, but I remember her," said Stanley

"We'll need to set up a play date with Alicia and Ruth," said Evelyn.

Ruth was horrified. She was too old for playdates organised by her grandmother and was about to speak when her father said, "That could be a good idea, Mother. I'll discuss it with Ruth later."

She was shocked he would say that, but when she looked at him, he gave her a wink, and she understood. They might need this if they find it difficult to make progress through the school.

Later, in Stanley's study, they sat on the floor, decompressing in silence. Finally, Stanley asked, "How was it?"

"Overwhelming but good," Ruth said. "The coursework is easy, but the culture... it's so layered. I thought a school full of Calaberra would feel uniform, but the diversity of personalities is wild."

Stanley smiled. "You've had a sheltered life until now. But you'll adapt. And you've got me, Conney, and Raymond in your corner."

"I know. And I'm looking forward to it," Ruth said, grinning. "How about you?"

"Ms. Ellis invited me to a parent group that meets fortnightly. And she's offering coaching on raising a teenager," Stanley said proudly.

"Look at us. Alliance heroes in the making," Ruth teased.

Stanley laughed. "We're off to a strong start. I'm proud of us."

"Me too," Ruth agreed, heading to bed with a satisfied smile. *Haleberry didn't know what was coming.*

Chapter 8
The Forum of Power:
Survival in the Social Minefield

When Stanley strolled into his first parent forum, the room buzzed with vibrant energy. The lively chatter bounced off the gilded walls like some bizarre symphony of privilege. Everyone looked youthful, radiant, unnervingly smooth-skinned—but Stanley knew better. Some of these "parents," like himself, were over a hundred, though you'd never guess it, thanks to the wonders of Gnia-itra. Age only mattered in commoner societies; in elite circles, no one aged.

Stanley's mission felt more like navigating a social minefield: meet as many parents as possible without seeming desperate, memorise their names for later research, and build a connection with the parents Raymond deemed essential. He hoped this would be easier for him than it was for Ruth, as today's focus was Arabella and Alicia's parents.

Arabella was identified as the niece of the newly appointed President Crumpt Junior, and Alicia was a member of the notorious Sherlock media empire. Raymond had said, "Building relationships with them would be invaluable to the Alliance. "

Stanley wasn't without his own profile. Inheriting his father's title and wealth and being a credible attorney meant he wasn't out of place. The downside was that their legal teams were often Stanley's opponents in court, so how he would be accepted remained to be seen. There was hope, though, as these people were so wealthy that losing the types of court cases he represented had no real impact on their wealth. They'd often say, "Well, it's just business," whereas to Stanley's clients, it was very personal.

Ms Ellis greeted him at the door, handing him a cocktail with a practised smile. "Welcome, Mr. Rossiter."

He surprised himself with how at ease he was circulating amongst them. He started with those he already knew and saved the Sherlocks and Crumpts for last so he could have more extended conversations with them. He was surprised they were there, but in hindsight, he realised they were there for the same reason: networking, albeit with very different agendas.

At one point, a woman he didn't recognise caught his attention. She stood with effortless grace. Her hair, a cascade of silver and grey, framed her face timelessly and defiantly. It was beautiful, not in the polished way of youth, but in the raw, elemental beauty that only age and experience could offer.

Her eyes, sharp and intense, shone with a passion that belied the calm exterior she wore. She was in the middle of an argument, her words flowing like a smooth, sharp, and powerful symphony. Her voice was loud but not harsh. It cut through the air like silk, each syllable landing with a delicate yet commanding weight. The contrast was striking: a voice that could lull someone into a sense of comfort one moment and cut to the heart of an issue the next.

She stood tall, her body relaxed but electric with energy. Her hands gestured as she spoke, painting pictures with her words. The fire in her expression was apparent: she wasn't just arguing; she was fighting for something she deeply believed in, and her conviction was as much a part of her as her wild, silver-streaked hair.

Her bohemian spirit, untamed and unfiltered, made her magnetic. She reminded Stanley of Janey, not so much in looks as in how she held herself and made her point.

Stanley didn't mean to eavesdrop, not obviously anyway. Still, he couldn't help but be intrigued by what they argued about. "How can you say that capitalism works? Have you not seen outside of these walls?" she asked the man that Stanley also didn't know.

"The system relies on paying workers less than the value they produce, which perpetuates class divides and ensures that the wealthy remain in control," Stanley wasn't sure if she heard the man respond.

"So," more a statement than a question was her opponent's response.

She continued, practically without a breath, "Companies prioritise short-term financial gain over long-term sustainability, contributing to environmental degradation, deforestation, pollution, and climate change."

Stanley didn't recognise the man but instantly disliked him. He smirked. "Anna, if you mean *my company*, we're establishing eco-communities that ensure sustainability."

Seeing his window of opportunity shrink as the debate escalated, Stanley interrupted. "Interesting discussion you two are having," he remarked.

Two sets of sharp eyes swung his way, both equally unimpressed. For a moment, Stanley wondered if he'd just made the biggest mistake of the evening.

The woman took a deep breath while Stanley introduced himself.

The man's face lit up with recognition. "Stanley Rossiter! We've crossed paths before—you represented the Albersteen community against my company. Alan Caldwell." He thrust out a hand with all the grace of a wrecking ball.

Stanley shifted his gaze from the woman to Alan. He hadn't recognised Alan, as they'd never met in person, but he knew him and his company well." Stanley would have rejected the man's hand if he hadn't been at the forum with a purpose, but he knew he had to accept his greeting and shake it. Although he couldn't help himself by saying, "I can't say I have been looking forward to meeting you."

As soon as he said it, he realised Alan had taken it as a compliment, thinking Stanley feared him rather than despising him for his actions. Losing the case was a significant blow to Stanley and the community he represented. Due to a new policy introduced by the Crumpt government, Alan's company could forcibly buy all the community's land, and the community had no choice but to work for Caldwell Industries.

Alan moved quickly to pat Stanley on the back, thinking he was putting him at ease, "I hope there aren't any hard feelings; it's just business." he said, laughing.

Stanley couldn't bring himself to agree or show he accepted the appalling outcome of the case, so he said in a neutral voice, "It was a tough case,"

Then, not wanting to discuss the case with this person, Stanley turned to the woman and said, "I don't think we have met. "

Alan, speaking with a familiarity that annoyed Stanley, said, "This is Anna Sherlock; she is Alexandra's mother."

Although Stanley knew he was supposed to move to the more powerful Crumpts and Sherlocks, he felt he could justify engaging in conversation with Anna as she was a Sherlock. It was strange, but he knew he wouldn't want to end any conversation he started with Anna. He hoped Alan would move away but resigned to the fact that it was beneficial to engage with them both at the same time. As he observed, Anna could challenge Alan in ways he shouldn't.

Even though he hadn't discussed it with Raymond, Stanley knew that a relationship with Alan would benefit the Alliance. It was childish of him not to take this opportunity because he hated the man.

"Nice to meet you, Anna," said Stanley.

Nodding, Anna said, "Same. I'm familiar with your work, particularly Alan's case, which I'm sorry you lost."

Stanley wasn't quite sure how to respond. He would've loved to discuss the case with her but didn't want to get Alan offside. He didn't need to worry, though, because Alan, being so self-absorbed, jumped in. He told them how close he had been to Anna's grandfather and how he was one of the new President's closest confidants.

"Here, let me show you," grabbing Stanley's arm and dragging him across the room to introduce him to the President. Stanley couldn't have been more disappointed if he had been told his fly was undone, but he knew it was an opportunity he couldn't turn down.

So, in the motion of being dragged, he managed to turn to Anna and give her a wave and a shrug. She smiled and gave a little wave.

President Crumpt was in conversation when Alan abruptly stopped beside him. Alan didn't even wait for the person he was talking to to stop talking before interjecting.

"Donald, this is Stanley, Evelyn Rossiter's son," said Alan.

Stanley braced himself as the President turned, irritation flickering across his face before being replaced by a politician's grin. "Stanley! I knew your father well. Shame we haven't met before."

Stanley tried not to show surprise, "Yes, I've kept a low profile over the past few decades,"

"What brings you to this forum," the President's companion asked.

"My daughter, Ruth, moved to this school last week," he responded.

"Where was she before," the President asked.

"At a Montessori school, but we thought it was time she moved to a more modern environment," said Stanley.

"Well, good choice, I hope that means we will see you more involved in our networks," said the President

"Yes, I've decided I need to be more active in the community," he responded.

"Well, good for you," said the President.

The small talk that followed was smooth, calculated, and entirely draining. When Stanley made it home, the tension he'd been holding all night finally broke. Collapsing into his study with a stiff drink, he laughed—part relief, part disbelief. Networking, it seemed, was a blood sport, and tonight, he'd survived the arena.

Chapter 9
Mission Undercover:
Father-Daughter Dynamics

The following morning, Ruth practically bounced down the hall to her father's wing, buzzing with excitement. She rang the bell to his rooms, still in his pyjamas, he opened the door, blinking at her like she was an apparition. He couldn't remember the last time she'd voluntarily ventured into his rooms. Was this what parenting success felt like?

Despite the pyjamas, Stanley had shaved and was halfway through dressing when Ruth surprised him. She was clearly revealing in their new father-daughter spy dynamic.

"Well?" she asked, plopping herself onto his armchair. "How was it? Did you meet their parents? Spill"

Stanley, still slightly dazed, managed a grin. "Yes, actually. It went exceedingly well. I surprised myself—I talked to *so many* people." His voice brimmed with an enthusiasm that caught even him off guard.

He launched into a high-level debrief, describing the who's who of the room and the kinds of conversations swirling around. Ruth listened intently, her eyes sparkling with curiosity.

"Do you know an Alexandra?" he asked at one point.

"There are a few. What's Alexandra's last name?"

"Sherlock," he replied.

"Yeah, she is one of the goths, but I haven't spoken to her yet. She seems very quiet. Should I?" Ruth asked.

"I think that might be a good idea," Stanley said, more for selfish reasons than for the Alliance, he thought guiltily.

"Okay, but did you talk to Alicia and Arabella's parents?"

Stanley sighed, half proud, half exasperated. "I was briefly introduced to Kalan—Alicia's father. He was in the middle of telling a group about some extravagant trip when I met him. He kept talking, so I didn't get a word in."

"Well, that's a start," Ruth said, sounding very much like the commander of their spy operation.

"I did, however, have a longer, though superficial, conversation with the President and Arabella's mother," Stanley continued. "They were together when I was introduced. They didn't look thrilled to be interrupted. But they were polite, of course, they're both politicians. It turns out the President knows my mother and had known my father well, and he encouraged me to get more involved in their networks."

Ruth's eyes widened. "Wow, Dad! That's great progress for your first undercover mission!"

Stanley laughed at the absurdity of it all. Being a spy sounded so out of character, which he knew was why he was useful to the Alliance.

They had already agreed that Ruth wouldn't push too hard with Alicia and Arabella at school due to their high profiles and popularity; access was difficult. "Play it cool" was their motto—try to build relationships with them outside school first, where the stakes were lower and teenage politics wouldn't interfere. This was where Stanley's ability to access their parents was helpful.

"Okay," Ruth said decisively. "Today, I'll scope out Alexandra. See if there's a natural way to get closer to her."

"Excellent," said Stanley, a little too excitedly. "Do you know a Caldwell?"

"We haven't spoken, but I know who it would be: Thomas Caldwell, " she said.

"He's hard to miss. Football team captain and a photographer for the senior school's newspaper. In our research, Conney and I were surprised that someone in middle school would be given the opportunity to publish their photos in the senior's newspaper. I guess it's because his photos are really good," she continued.

"Interesting," Stanley muttered. "Be cautious with him. His father is… the devil."

Ruth blinked, taken aback. "Wow, okay, Dad. That's a bit dramatic—even for you. What did he do?"

Stanley sighed, the weight of the memory visible on his face. "He took over an entire community. I was representing them in court, trying to stop him, but he lobbied for a law change that let him legally *own* a community. It was devastating for the people—and the precedent it set? Dangerous."

Ruth's face shifted, her playful demeanour replaced with determination. "Sounds like someone I *need* to get to know."

Stanley's face darkened. "I'm not sure I'm comfortable with that."

"Trust me, Dad," she said with a grin, rising from the chair and heading for the door.

Before she left, Stanley pulled her into a tight hug. "Be careful, Ruth."

"I will," she replied, rolling her eyes just a little. But as she walked away, Stanley couldn't help but feel both proud and utterly terrified.

Returning to her room, Ruth dove headfirst into Conney's notes on goth culture, revising like a student cramming for an exam. She flipped through the scribbled pages, a mix of insightful observations and questionable guesses.

Ruth glanced at the playlist she'd curated, mentally patting herself on the back for her recent deep dive into moody music. She'd added "A Fragile Thing" by The Cure and "In the Morning We'll Be Someone Else" by Midas Fall, hoping those were staples in the goth repertoire. But she couldn't shake the feeling. It was all a bit of a shot in the dark.

What if Alexandra's taste leaned more towards obscure underground techno? Or worse, mainstream pop? Goths were a minefield of contradictions, and Ruth was tiptoeing through it blindfolded.

Then, there was *the book* they had ordered. Ruth pulled it off her shelf with a mixture of pride and trepidation. *Red X* by David Demchuk. Queer horror. A niche within a niche, obscure enough to earn goth credibility—or so she hoped. Ruth slid the book into her school bag, trying to channel the mysterious, brooding energy she imagined Alexandra and her crew might radiate.

Sure, *Red X* was a wild card—it was older and didn't scream "current goth trend"—but it had the kind of weird, unsettling vibe Ruth thought might catch the right attention. If nothing else, it was unique, and isn't that what goths thrived on? The plan was simple: carry the book around school and hope it acted like a goth Bat-Signal. If Alexandra noticed and initiated a conversation, Ruth would be ready to swoop in, full of pseudo-goth coolness and just enough quirk to sell it.

She slung her bag over her shoulder and headed out, hoping that her playlist, book, and whatever goth-adjacent energy she could muster would be enough to crack the code of Alexandra's mysterious world.

Still riding high on Ruth's energy and determined to keep the momentum going from last evening, Stanley mulled over his next move. The President's casual encouragement to "get more involved in the networks" echoed in his head. Sure, it sounded like small talk, but Stanley knew better—opportunities were lurking in those words. He just needed a game plan; for that, he'd need Raymond.

Stanley decided he couldn't wait until their next scheduled meeting. He activated the code they'd agreed on for covert communication: an innocent-sounding invitation for Raymond to "discuss his will" in Stanley's office. Perfectly mundane on the surface, it was the kind of cover story that wouldn't raise an eyebrow. After all, what could be more ordinary than a lawyer chatting with his client about estate planning?

Stanley smiled to himself, appreciating the layers of precaution they'd taken. His office was regularly swept for bugs. It was a fortress of attorney-client privilege, dressed up as an unassuming workspace. If anyone asked, he was just a lawyer offering stellar legal advice—

not a man navigating the labyrinth of high-stakes political alliances.

He hit send and leaned back in his chair, feeling a strange thrill at the absurdity of it all and planning clandestine strategy meetings disguised as legal appointments. That wasn't part of his law school curriculum. But here he was, playing the game, one carefully coded message at a time.

Chapter 10
Web of Deceit:
The Alliance Unveiled

Raymond arrived precisely at the appointed time, stepping into Stanley's office with his usual air of calm competence. But even he couldn't miss the change in Stanley's demeanour. The man was standing straighter, moving with an energy Raymond hadn't seen before, and—was that a smile? Raymond was genuinely thrown. Stanley smiling was like spotting a unicorn in a suit.

Once seated, Stanley immediately began recounting the events of the previous evening, including his interactions with various people and his spirited morning debrief with Ruth. He felt a small surge of pride when Raymond nodded thoughtfully and said, "I think Ruth getting close to Alexandra is a solid plan. And you should absolutely start building a relationship with Anna."

Stanley tried, and mostly failed, to suppress a grin. "Should I wait until Ruth and Alexandra are on good terms, or should I make contact with Anna now?"

Raymond waved a hand dismissively. "Let's give Ruth the week to see how things progress. We'll revisit the idea at our next meeting."

Then Raymond leaned back, looking thoughtful. "In the meantime, send follow-up notes to everyone you met last evening, including the President and Anna. Just polite, professional messages—'pleasure to meet you' or 'reconnect,' whatever fits. Let's see if anything useful shakes loose from that."

Just as he thought the meeting was wrapping up, Raymond leaned forward, his expression sharpening.

"There's someone I want you to meet," he said. "But I cannot stress this enough: her relationship with the Alliance must remain confidential. Exposing her would be disastrous—not just for us, but for her and her family."

Stanley straightened in his chair, feeling the weight of the task. "Of course. Should I treat her as if she's just another client?"

"Exactly," Raymond said. "She'll make an appointment, like any new client. Her name is Moira Hemingway."

Stanley blinked. "Percy's daughter? Jonathon's wife?"

Raymond nodded. "Yes. Now you understand why secrecy is critical. She and her husband, Jonathon, are deeply connected to the Alliance. She has valuable insights about the people you met last night."

Stanley nodded again, though his brain was spinning. "I'll make sure my secretary sets something up."

"No," Raymond said quickly. "She'll contact you, just like a regular client. It can't look staged."

With that, Raymond rose, shook Stanley's hand, and left.

For the next three days, Stanley couldn't stop checking his calendar, obsessively refreshing it like a teenager waiting for a crush's text. Finally, the appointment appeared: Moira Hemingway, scheduled for a day before his next meeting with Raymond.

When she arrived, Stanley greeted her with his best client-friendly smile. "Nice to meet you, Moira. Please, come in and have a seat."

"Thank you," Moira said, easing into the chair with the careful grace of someone very pregnant. "I'm getting so tired these days."

"Of course," Stanley said, immediately shifting into host mode. "Can I get you some water?"

"No, thank you," she said with a polite smile. "I'm fine."

Stanley sat down, ready to get to business. "I understand you're here to provide details about key people in the Calaberra and answer any questions I might have. Is this your understanding?"

Moira nodded. "That's right. But first, I'd like to hear more about you. What brought you to the Alliance?"

Stanley blinked. He wasn't expecting an interview. "I'll need a drink for that," he said, half-joking, as he poured himself a scotch—a rare indulgence for him during the workday.

He recounted his journey, Janey's role in pulling him into the Alliance, and Ruth's growing involvement. As he spoke, Moira listened intently, her eyes searching for signs of sincerity.

By the end, she seemed satisfied. "Thank you for sharing that. I wanted to ensure I could trust you before giving you details that could expose people I consider friends."

Feeling more comfortable, Stanley leaned forward. "Your turn, then. Tell me about yourself—and your family, if you don't mind."

Moira smiled faintly and launched into her story, tracing her family's history back to her grandmother's controversial experiments and the unintended consequences of her parents' work on the longevity drug and the late-term pregnancy program. Stanley was riveted, hanging on every word. Her tale was part science, part intrigue, and entirely captivating. By the end, he felt he'd known her and Jonathon for years.

"Do you have any questions about my family or the science?" Moira asked when she finished.

Stanley shook his head, still processing. "I'm sure I will later, but for now, I just want to absorb everything you've told me."

"Fair enough," she said. "Shall we move on to the people you met last night?"

"Yes, please," Stanley said, eager to dive into her insights. Moira smiled knowingly, ready to share secrets that could reshape his understanding of the network he was trying to navigate.

Knowing the faces of the people, Moira's insights added a chilling weight to her revelations. As she unravelled the web of connections, it became clear that Alan wasn't just a charismatic figurehead—he was the polished tip of a spear aimed at dismantling entire communities. Behind him loomed a much larger, insidious plan set in motion decades ago, quietly advancing under the guise of progress.

The Crumpt government, Moira explained with both urgency and frustration, had laid the groundwork for this scheme long before anyone realised its full implications. Their vision was as bold as it was ruthless: to package and commodify every community that fell outside their neatly defined "Calaberra cities," hollowing them out for profit. Worse still, they had crafted a veneer of legitimacy by cloaking their motives in policies that touted "environmental sustainability" as their justification. In reality, these policies were nothing more than a smoke screen—a cynical coverup for a land grab driven by unrestrained greed.

Stanley felt his chest tighten as he pieced it together. The so-called purchases, framed as benevolent investments in the planet's future, were, in truth, a calculated erosion of autonomy for these communities. Entire livelihoods would be consumed under the guise of a green agenda, leaving nothing but a trail of broken promises and imprisoned people. It wasn't just a betrayal—it was a blueprint for exploitation on a staggering scale.

Moira's voice wavered slightly as she continued, her passion laced with concern. "They've spent years perfecting this strategy, Stanley. The policies, the propaganda, and the handpicked spokespeople like Alan are all part of a machine designed to make it seem inevitable, even beneficial. But it's not. It's theft, pure and simple."

Stanley nodded slowly, his mind racing. The stakes were far higher than he'd realised, and the faces of those he had met the previous evening now carried a heavier, more sinister weight. These weren't just power players— they were architects of a future Stanley was sure he didn't want. And somehow, he and Ruth were now standing at the edge of it, tasked with finding a way to push back before it was too late.

Chapter 11
Fate, Games and New Beginnings

Ruth, determined but slightly flustered, was still trying to catch Alexandra's attention when fate intervened in a way she hadn't planned. Her grand idea—following Alexandra into the bathroom armed with a carefully chosen goth-bait book—seemed solid in theory. Ruth had staged the book on the washbasin like an offering to the goth gods and slipped into a stall, ready to make her move, when Alexandra inevitably noticed the literary gem while washing her hands.

But Ruth's timing was off. When she emerged, trying to look casual yet approachable, Alexandra was already heading for the door. Ruth opened her mouth to say something—anything—but the bathroom door burst open before she could, and someone else barged in.

Determined to salvage the moment, Ruth washed her hands with speed bordering on desperation and flung the door open with gusto, only to crash directly into someone. Her bag and the book went flying in a dramatic mess.

"Oh my gosh, I'm so sorry!" she blurted, crouching to pick up her things—until she realised who she'd just collided with. Standing before her, smiling effortlessly, was none other than *Thomas Caldwell*. The school's golden boy, football captain, amateur photographer, and the kind of guy you don't expect to literally run into in a bathroom blind spot.

"It's okay," Thomas said with a grin, bending to help retrieve her things. "I should've been more careful. This is a blind spot, after all."

Ruth blinked. *Who apologises for standing in a blind spot?* She thought, thrown off by his kindness.

When Thomas stood, he was holding her book. "Huh," he said, inspecting the cover. "I've never seen this one before. What's it about?"

"Oh, uh…" Ruth stammered, scrambling for words. "It's, um, kind of... a queer horror story. You know, really niche."

Thomas raised an eyebrow, clearly intrigued. "Interesting. I like diverse literature. Do you?"

Ruth straightened up, trying to appear as composed as someone who wasn't swooning.

"Yeah, totally. I try to read a bit of everything."

He handed her book and bag back, nodding thoughtfully. "Huh," he said again before waving and jogging off, leaving Ruth standing there clutching the book like it was a talisman of fate.

Her first interaction with Thomas Caldwell was entirely accidental and unplanned, and it made her heart flutter. She wasn't sure if it counted as progress in her mission or just a random twist of fate, but she didn't have time to overanalyse.

At the end of the day, she found a note tucked into her locker. Her heart nearly exploded as she read:

"Hi, new girl. You should come to the game on Saturday."

It was signed: *Thomas (Red X).*

Ruth was flattered beyond belief. No boy had ever approached her before—let alone *this* boy. Thomas Caldwell is a star athlete and a bona fide school legend. She tried to rationalise the situation, telling herself, *This is perfect for the mission!* But deep down, a giddy giggle bubbled up that would've horrified any goth on principle.

The game was fortuitous for both Ruth and Stanley. Ruth could try her luck with Alexandra, while Stanley might connect with Anna. He messaged Anna, asking if she and Alexandra would be attending. To his surprise, she replied yes, and even invited him and Ruth to sit with them.

Stanley couldn't have planned it better if he'd tried.

At the game, Ruth managed to strike up a conversation with Alexandra, her determination finally paying off. Meanwhile, Stanley's exchanges with Anna were polite but limited, leaving him unsure how to proceed. His focus shifted, however, when he overheard the woman next to Anna whisper, "Did you hear about Moira? Poor Jonathan."

Anna sighed deeply. "Yes, it's so sad. That poor baby. I'm helping Jonathan with the arrangements."

Stanley's ears perked up. "What happened to Moira?" he asked.

Anna turned to him in surprise. "You knew her?"

"She was a client," Stanley said, his voice faltering. "I met her for the first time last week. She seemed so... alive."

Anna's face softened. "She delivered a beautiful baby girl but had complications and didn't survive the surgery. It's why the teams are wearing black armbands today."

Stanley was stunned. He mumbled an apology and excused himself, finding a quiet spot to call Raymond.

"Raymond," he began, his voice thick with emotion, "did you hear about Moira?"

"Yes," Raymond said solemnly. "It's devastating. We're still trying to understand what happened."

"Do you think it was because of her connection to... the Alliance?" Stanley asked hesitantly.

"No, we don't believe so," Raymond replied. "But we can't take chances. Just continue as normal, Stanley. I'm sorry I didn't tell you earlier—it's been chaos here."

Stanley nodded, even though Raymond couldn't see him. "Of course. Take care, Raymond."

When Stanley returned to his seat, Anna immediately noticed his sombre expression. "You seem sad, Stanley. Now I understand why."

"I'm sorry," she added gently. "If I'd known you knew Moira, I would've told you sooner."

Stanley shook his head. "How could you have known? It's fine—well, it's not fine, but you know what I mean."

Anna placed her hand on his, her touch unexpectedly comforting. "I do, Stanley," she said, her voice steady and kind. "Let's focus on the girls and the game for now. We can figure out how to support Jonathan and his new baby later."

Stanley felt a pang of something he hadn't expected—a flutter in his chest. It wasn't just her words but how she'd said *'we'* that lingered in his mind, a flicker of warmth amid the sorrow.

The game was electrifying, every moment gripping as Haleberry fought for the win. When the final siren blared, declaring victory by a single point, the crowd erupted in a frenzy of cheers and celebration. The excitement was palpable, but Stanley's mind was elsewhere, already scanning the crowd with a protective parent's vigilance.

As they headed out of the stands, Ruth tugged on his sleeve, her eyes bright with exhilaration. "Dad, Alexandra's going to the after-party. Can I go, please?"

His gut reaction was to say no. The thought of Ruth, still new to this world, diving into a high school party with unfamiliar faces set off alarm bells. But before he could respond, Anna chimed in, her voice calm and reassuring.

"I'm dropping Alexandra off and picking her up," Anna said warmly. "I'd be happy to do the same for Ruth. There's no alcohol allowed, and the parents of the house will be home the entire time."

Stanley hesitated, glancing between Anna's steady gaze and Ruth's hopeful expression. How could he refuse? But the worry gnawed at him. This wasn't just about safety—it was about trust, about letting Ruth navigate an environment he couldn't control.

"Okay," he said at last, his voice firm but tinged with concern. "But you stick with Alexandra, understand? Stay together."

Ruth nodded eagerly, but his words weren't just an undercover directive—they came from the heart of a worried father. This was all new to Ruth: the people, the parties, the social currents she'd have to navigate. Stanley couldn't help but feel like he was sending her into unknown waters, hoping she'd stay afloat.

As they parted ways, Stanley's eyes lingered on Ruth. He wanted to trust her, but the unease in his chest wouldn't quiet. For her, this might have been an exciting chance to blend in. For him, it was an exercise in faith—and a silent prayer for her to come back unscathed.

Chapter 12
The Night Unfolds

Moira's death was devastating in so many ways. A talented, vibrant woman gone. Raymond said that Jonathon, although not outrightly blaming her death on their relationship with the Alliance, said that he would no longer take part in any of the Alliance's activities. He wants to protect his daughter and feels that would be the best way.

It was a significant loss to all, but Stanley could easily understand Jonathon's position.

For Ruth, she found the party a little more vibrant than she had expected; there were teenagers spread out everywhere, and the music was very loud. Alexandra disappeared within minutes of their arrival, leaving Ruth to fend for herself.

Not knowing what else to do, she gravitated to an empty corner of the main lounge, where most of the dancing was taking place. She tried to blend into the wallpaper, clutching her drink as a prop. Her eyes scan the crowd for Alexandra or anyone she vaguely recognises.

A tall figure emerged from the chaos before she could spot a friendly face and approached her. His movements were deliberate, almost predatory. "Hi, I'm Jack," he said in a voice so low it was practically a growl.

"Ruth," she replied, her unease sharpening.

He didn't smile, didn't offer small talk. Instead, his dark eyes fixed on Ruth with unnerving intensity. "I haven't seen you around before."

"I've always lived in the area," she said, forcing herself to sound casual. "I just transferred to Haleberry."

Before she could process his reaction, he moved closer. Too close. His hand brushed against her back, his chest pressing into hers, trapping her against the wall. The sudden invasion of her space set off every alarm in her mind.

At first, she tried to calculate how to handle the situation for her mission—what a typical Haleberry teen might do. But when his lips found her neck, her mind emptied of strategy and filled with panic.

"Get off me!" she said, her voice cracking with fear as she pushed against him.

Jack's grip tightened, his breath hot against her ear. "Oh, come on. You like this. I know you do," he whispered, his tone dripping with menace. "Struggle more if you want; it just makes it better."

Her heart pounded in terror. She twisted and pushed with all her strength, but he was relentless, his grip a vice, his presence suffocating. Just as her panic peaked, he was suddenly yanked away, the pressure disappearing like a snapped rubber band.

"Hey, man, she obviously doesn't like what you're doing. Back off," said a familiar, firm, and commanding voice.

Ruth's wide eyes focused on her unexpected saviour—Thomas Caldwell.

Jack muttered something under his breath, his bravado shrinking under Thomas's glare, and slinked back into the crowd.

Ruth stood there, shaken, her heart still hammering in her chest. She stared at Thomas, unsure which was more shocking: Jack's predatory behaviour or that Thomas, the golden boy of Haleberry, had come to her rescue.

"You okay?" Thomas asked gently, his earlier bravado replaced with genuine concern.

Ruth nodded mutely, her throat too tight to speak. She wasn't sure she'd be okay again after what had just happened. But for now, she was safe.

"Alexandra said you were coming, so I was looking out for you. I'm sorry that happened. You must think we're all a bunch of Neanderthals," he said glumly.

She had started to regain her composure, and realising how much he regretted what had happened, she said, "I'm definitely not used to that kind of person. At first, I thought I could handle it, but obviously, now... Thank you."

"Please don't thank me. I was just glad I was around," he said

Ruth's mind was spinning in circles. Thomas seemed so... nice. Friendly, even. But her dad's grim description of his father painted a very different picture. She needed time to figure him out.

"Wanna sit by the pool? It's quieter out there," Thomas offered, flashing an easy grin.

"Uh, okay," Ruth said hesitantly, following as he expertly navigated the throng of dancers. She trailed behind him, relieved when they finally stepped into the cool night air. She inhaled deeply, grateful for a moment to reset her frazzled nerves.

Thomas sensed her unease launching into small talk. "So, what did you think of the game?"

"Well," she admitted, "I didn't understand most of it. I just watched the scoreboard and cheered when everyone else did. But when it got close, I thought I would throw up from nerves!"

He chuckled. "That's one way to watch it. Did you at least notice me throwing the ball?" "Oh, I noticed. You got hit. A lot. Are you okay?"

"Sure, that's just part of the game. I'm used to it," Thomas said with a shrug, like being tackled by angry linebackers was no big deal.

"If it were me, I'd be in traction. I wouldn't be walking, let alone at a party. Are you sure you're okay?" Ruth pressed, genuinely incredulous.

"Totally fine. It's what we train for," he said, clearly enjoying her disbelief. "Sounds like I'll need to teach you the rules so you can follow the action better at our next home game."

"Oh, so now I'm your student?" she teased, raising an eyebrow. "How often do you guys even play?"

"Every week, though not always at home."

"And you put your body through that every week? You must be made of titanium or something."

He laughed. "I wish. But we've got protective gear. The helmets might look flimsy, but they're reinforced with repropcure. We're pretty safe these days."

"Well, that's a relief," Ruth said, smiling.

Thomas returned her smile, and for a moment, everything else faded—the noise, the party, the mission—just his warm and unassuming smile.

Before she knew it, time had flown by, and Alexandra appeared, looking frazzled. "Time to go. Mum is on her way," she announced, then added with a deadpan, "Oh, hi, Thomas."

Ruth stood, reluctantly leaving the little bubble of calm they'd found. "Thanks for helping me out earlier," she said.

"See you at school," Thomas replied casually, watching her leave.

Alexandra turned as they walked through the house, her eyes narrowing with suspicion. "What's going on with you two?"

"Nothing," Ruth said quickly. "He just helped me out of a tight spot."

This caught Alexandra's attention. "What tight spot?"

Ruth explained. And Alexandra didn't miss a beat as they passed Jack on the dance floor. She stuck out her foot, tripping him flat on his face.

"What the hell? Why did you do that?" Jack sputtered, glaring up at her.

"Just because you're a jerk," Alexandra shot back before striding off with Ruth in tow.

Standing out front waiting for the car, Ruth noticed Alexandra seemed unusually quiet. "Hey, is everything okay? You don't need to worry about Jack and me. I know he's not worth it."

"It's not that. He *is* a jerk, though," Alexandra muttered.

"Then what is it?" Ruth asked.

Alexandra hesitated before groaning. "It's my stupid boyfriend. He got so drunk he passed out. Ugh."

Ruth blinked, unsure how to respond. "Uh... I'm sorry?"

"Hi, Dad! I'm home," Ruth chirped, slapping on her best 'happy to be here' smile.

Before she could say another word, he hugged her tightly, holding on like she might disappear.

"Uh, okay," she said, her voice muffled against his shoulder. "I'm home, safe and sound. You can stop worrying now."

He didn't let go. "I know, sweetheart. I just… I needed a hug tonight."

She leaned back to look at him, her concern breaking through the cheer. "What's wrong? Do you want to talk about it?"

"No, no," he said, releasing her and waving the thought away. "Forget about me. How was the party?"

Ruth hesitated, then decided to keep things light. "It started pretty miserably, but it ended... surprisingly great. I actually had a good time."

"Great, great, great," Stanley said, nodding emphatically, though his tone sounded distracted. His mind was clearly elsewhere.

"Okay, Dad. Well, goodnight," Ruth said, lingering for a moment before heading toward the stairs.

As she walked to her room, she felt a slight glow of happiness at how the evening had turned around, but a twinge of worry for her father lingered. Whatever had shaken him, he wasn't ready to share it just yet.

Chapter 13
The Weight of Regret

Stanley lay in his sanctuary, the warm cocoon of his bed finally giving him the solitude he needed to fall apart. The day's weight pressed down on him, and the dam broke, releasing a flood of tears. It wasn't just about Moira; her loss ignited everything he'd been suppressing.

A century of life, and what had he done with it? He'd been an observer, watching the world twist and turn, evolve and decay, but not fully stepping in to shape it. How had he allowed the world to become so cruel, so indifferent to the struggles of the common people?

And then there was Janey. The memory of her was like shards of glass cutting through him. He could see her as clearly as if she were standing before him: fierce, determined, tirelessly striving to make the world better. She had fought with every fibre of her being while he… he had stood in the shadows, watching her burn herself out. He could have done more. He *should* have done more.

Even after she was gone, he had the chance to honour her legacy and continue her work. But instead, he'd let the world carry him along like a piece of driftwood, passive and inert. And now people like Moira—people who should have been basking in the joy of new life, preparing to raise their children in safety and hope—were left fighting battles they shouldn't have faced.

Stanley's hands clenched the blanket as sobs wracked his body. He wasn't just mourning Moira, or Janey, or the life he could never have again. He was mourning the man he should have been—the man he still *needed* to become. The weight of his failures pressed down on him, yet within it was a glimmer of something else.

Resolve.

The guilt wasn't just a punishment but a reminder, a call to action. Stanley couldn't undo the past, but he could damn well shape the future. For Moira. For Janey. For everyone still fighting to live in a world that didn't seem to care.

When Stanley finally fell asleep, his pillow was soaked, but his resolve was ironclad. By the time the morning sun broke through his window, he was already formulating a plan. He arrived at his office with an energy he hadn't felt in decades, tearing through Moira's notes, searching for threads to follow, excuses to reconnect with the key players. He would help push the Alliance forward, bit by bit, using every resource at his disposal.

This time, Janey's voice echoed in his mind softer, warmer: *"That's more like it, Stanley."*

He smirked, a bitter laugh escaping his lips. "Better late than never, right, Janey?" And with that, he threw himself into the work.

Barron Crumpt, the President's enigmatic brother, had always intrigued Stanley. Moira had warmly praised him, mentioning how she and Jonathon had forged a friendship with him. According to her, Barron genuinely cared about uplifting the common people—a rarity in circles of power.

Barron hadn't attended the parent forum, but there was another connection: his granddaughter, Juliette, was Ruth's age. That link alone presented an opportunity. What's more, Stanley already had a professional history with Barron. Their paths had crossed several times when Barron, an acclaimed chemist, had served as an expert witness in some of Stanley's most complex cases. While their interactions had primarily been professional, Stanley had always admired Barron's intellect and unflappable demeanour. There had been moments of mutual respect, but nothing that could be called a true friendship.

Still, the pieces were there—a shared history, a tangential connection through their children, and Moira's implicit trust in Barron's character. If Barron's interest in supporting the common good was genuine, this could be a golden opportunity to forge a deeper alliance.

Stanley's mind raced with possibilities. Using their shared history as a starting point, it seemed like a doorway waiting to be opened.

With renewed focus, Stanley drafted an invitation to lunch. He would tread carefully, balancing the personal with the strategic. If Barron indeed shared their values, he could be a powerful ally. If not? Well, Stanley would find out soon enough.

"Let's see how genuine you are, Barron," Stanley muttered to himself, feeling the fire of possibility as he wrote the invitation.

***

"Dear Barron,

It's been some time since we last spoke. Although our past interactions have been primarily professional, I've always felt there might be an opportunity for us to engage on a social level.

What prompted me to reach out is that Moira Pride (Hemingway) was a client of mine, and your name came up in our conversation.

She spoke warmly of you, and although I didn't know her well, I know her loss must be a significant blow to you.

I'm wondering if you'd like to have lunch sometime. We can talk shop, about Moira or whatever you prefer. I would appreciate the company.

Regards,

Stanley"

***

To Stanley's surprise, a response came back within half an hour.

***

"Hello Stanley,

I appreciate hearing a friendly voice during this difficult time. Yes, Moira and Jonathon are friends of mine, and her loss is hard to comprehend.

Jonathon is beside himself, and I'm unsure how to help him.

I would appreciate the opportunity to have lunch with you, though I must warn you that I won't be in an upbeat frame of mind, which I'm sure you understand.

Please pick a time and place, and I will rearrange my schedule to meet with you.

Thank you for your consideration.

Kind regards,

Barron"

***

Stanley felt a glimmer of hope. Barron's willingness to meet was a positive sign. With renewed determination, he began planning their lunch, intent on forging a connection that could change everything.

Raymond could not meet in person, so they spoke briefly over a secure connection.

"I've set up a meeting with Barron Crumpt. We have some history, and Moira spoke highly of him," Stanley said urgently.

"That's great news. With Moira gone and Jonathon pulling back, it's crucial to keep the conversation going with him," Raymond responded.

"Is he an Alliance member?" Stanley inquired.

"We're hopeful in the future, but you must proceed cautiously. Moira and Jonathon had just started discussing sensitive topics with him. We don't think he knew about their relationship with the Alliance, but she was close to revealing it. So, don't bring it up just yet—feel him out first," Raymond advised.

"Understood. Is there anything I can do to support Jonathon? Should I reach out?" Stanley asked.

"I wouldn't do anything for now. Focus on building rapport with Barron, and it may happen naturally, which would be all the better," Raymond replied.

"That makes sense. Also, his granddaughter is Ruth's age, so there might be an opportunity there, too," Stanley added.

"One step at a time. Start with the lunch, and then we'll talk," Raymond said before disconnecting.

Stanley's sense of urgency fuelled his resolve. The stakes were high, and he knew this lunch could be significant.

Chapter 14
A Dance of Strategy and Serendipity

Barron was already seated when Stanley arrived, looking every bit the picture of unbothered sophistication, sipping what was likely a too-expensive coffee. On the other hand, Stanley felt the weight of his plan pressing down on him as he stepped into the restaurant. He'd deliberately picked this spot—a bustling Calaberra haunt—because he wanted to be seen. If his face became familiar socialising with people like Barron Crumpt, it would help make his renewed entry into society less obvious. Or so he hoped.

He adjusted his tie and straightened his shoulders before striding toward the table. As he approached, Barron looked up, offering a small smile that seemed equal parts polite and mildly amused. It was as if he already knew Stanley's grand strategy and found it charmingly transparent.

Not naturally inclined to casual chit-chat, Stanley had spent hours with Raymond rehearsing. They'd mapped out a strategy: start with light conversation, steer toward family ties, and let Barron lead when Moira inevitably came up. Most importantly, Stanley was to listen, empathise, and keep his cards close to his chest. As a lawyer, Stanley was an excellent listener and prided himself on his ability to read people. However, the stakes were much higher when it was a personal rather than a legal endeavour.

If Barron suspected Stanley's connection to the Alliance, he didn't show it.

"So, how's your family?" Stanley began casually. "My daughter Ruth mentioned that she and your granddaughter Juliette are at the same school."

This started a safe conversation about the school system that continued through the entrees.

Then, just as the main course was being placed on the table, Barron's expression grew sombre. "Thank you for the distraction," he said quietly. "It's been hard to think about anything other than Moira. Her passing… and poor Jonathon left alone to care for a new baby. It's just so heavy."

Stanley nodded, his heart aching at the thought. "I can only imagine how difficult it is for him. Losing someone like Moira… it's a wound that doesn't heal."

Barron studied him for a moment. "You'd know something about that, wouldn't you? Losing Janey must've been unbearable."

Stanley's throat tightened, but he forced a small smile. "It was. But talking about her helps. Especially with Ruth. It's good to keep her memory alive."

The conversation turned to Janey's work, and Stanley carefully steered it toward her advocacy efforts. Barron listened intently, nodding in agreement. "She sounds remarkable," he said. She is the kind of person who stands firm when the world pushes back. I think she and Moira would've gotten along."

Stanley's heart lifted slightly. "I think so too."

Sensing an opportunity, Stanley gently shifted gears. "How did you and Moira meet?"

Barron's face softened, a nostalgic smile creeping in. "Her father, Percy, was a close friend of my fathers—an extraordinary man. We spent hours debating science, ethics, and everything in between. Moira was always right there, her mind as sharp as her father's. We'd talk about experiments and innovations, especially water quality. She had a way of making even the most complex problems seem solvable. We've been friends ever since."

"It must've been wonderful," Stanley said, leaning in. "Being part of those conversations."

Barron nodded. "It was. Though, near the end of Percy's life, things got… tense. He and my father had some heated debates."

"About?" Stanley prompted.

Barron hesitated, then waved a hand dismissively. "The Gnia-itra drug. Its accessibility, its impact. But that's a conversation for another day."

"I'll hold you to that," Stanley grinned.

When their meals arrived, they ate in companionable silence. Just as they finished, Barron's phone buzzed. He glanced at it, his brow furrowing slightly. "I have to take this," he said, standing. Stanley, this was… pleasant. Let's do it again."

Stanley rose as well, offering a firm handshake. "I'll look forward to it."

As Barron exited the restaurant, Stanley sank back into his chair, feeling equal parts satisfied and nervous. The meeting had gone well, but this was only the beginning. If Barron was the ally Moira believed him to be, there was still a long road ahead. For now, though, Stanley allowed himself a small smile and ordered another coffee—overpriced, of course.

Although Ruth had been at her new school for a few weeks, frustration bubbled beneath the surface. Progress was agonisingly slow, especially compared to Stanley, who seemed to be thriving in his integration efforts. It wasn't a competition, but if it was, she felt like she was trailing miserably behind.

Her social wins were modest but meaningful. So far, Thomas was her only solid friend. Alexandra, however, was showing signs of thawing. Ruth had casually joined her and her group for lunch a couple of times. Now, when she entered the cafeteria, a seat was waiting for her at their table. Sure, most of the conversation revolved around music—most of which she pretended to know about with vigorous nodding—but progress was progress. And hope lingered on the horizon: her father had arranged for Alexandra and her mother to join them for brunch on Saturday. It was an event Ruth oscillated between dreading and eagerly anticipating.

Her friendship with Thomas was more complicated. Raymond and Stanley had made their concerns about the budding relationship very clear—well, as clear as men with awkward dad energy could make them. Ruth wasn't sure if Thomas was genuinely kind or just exceptionally good at hiding a dark, villainous streak inherited from his father. Either way, she treads cautiously, ever the undercover operative.

Thomas had invited her over to his house several times, but Ruth had deflected deftly, claiming her father had a rule: no visits without a proper introduction. As a result, their study sessions took place at her house, allowing Stanley to size him up like a prosecutor cross-examining a witness. The next session, however, would be at Thomas's house. The prospect filled Ruth with equal parts curiosity and dread.

The real challenge wasn't navigating social politics or family brunches—it was trying very hard not to get lost in Thomas's ridiculously good looks. His effortless charisma could knock down defences faster than a battering ram. But Ruth had a mission and was determined not to let her heart derail it.

She'd developed a system: always carry something. If Thomas reached for her hand, she'd feign the need to clutch whatever it was with both hands—textbooks, a water bottle, even a random stapler—like her life depended on it. Because deep down, she knew that if he held her hand, she wouldn't want to let go. And letting go of her focus? That was not an option.

For now, Ruth held onto her resolve. With Alexandra warming up, brunch around the corner, and the prospect of snooping—uh, studying—at Thomas's house, there was a glimmer of momentum. If she played her cards right, she might turn frustration into progress. And maybe, just maybe, figure out where Thomas really stood in this complicated chess game of alliances and secrets.

Chapter 15
Enter Brunch: Chaos, Cookies, and Chemistry

Stanley's heart pounded with a thrilling cocktail of anticipation and nervous energy as he prepared for brunch with Anna and Alexandra. He had planned this day down to the smallest detail, carefully choosing the time when his mother would be engrossed in her regular bridge game. This was his chance— one he wasn't about to let slip.

In the kitchen, the air buzzed with an electric tension. Unaccustomed to Stanley's intense scrutiny, the staff moved with a new sense of caution. He hovered like a conductor over an orchestra, ensuring every detail was flawless. Outwardly, he told himself it was about ensuring everything was perfect for the mission. But deep down, he knew the truth. He wanted Anna to like him and genuinely enjoy his and Ruth's company.

It had been years since he'd felt this kind of nervous excitement—Janey had been the last. The fluttering in his chest made him wonder if the mission had cracked him open to these feelings. Or was Anna simply extraordinary, the kind of person who could light up his world no matter when they met? Whatever the reason, he couldn't deny the surge of hope that filled him.

Meanwhile, Anna stood before her mirror, trying to tame the butterflies fluttering in her stomach. Socialising was her bread and butter—it had been drilled into her from childhood. Her family practically had *making people feel special* written into their DNA. In the early days, her father had demanded it of her, and she'd complied, flashing her polished smile like a trophy. But as she grew older, the shine wore off. What once felt like a skill started to feel like a con.

It wasn't until she broke away from her family's orbit that she learned to wield her charm for something meaningful. Instead of dazzling dinner guests, she used it to spotlight causes she cared deeply about. Her ability to work a room became a tool of purpose, and she'd grown proud of that.

Still, today felt... different. This brunch wasn't just another social engagement. It carried a weight she couldn't quite explain. Perhaps it was the simple fact that she wanted to be there for Stanley, who seemed to need a friend. Or maybe it was because she hadn't decided if she was ready to let him into her life.

Then, there was the matter of the invitation itself. She couldn't ignore the little voice in her head pointing out that this was the first time since her divorce that she'd accepted a meal invite from a man that wasn't work or charity-related. Friendship was the sole intention here, which felt novel and slightly bizarre.

As she smoothed her dress and gave herself a final once-over in the mirror, Anna couldn't help but chuckle. She couldn't deny the spark of curiosity—and okay, maybe a little excitement—at what the morning might bring. With a chuckle, she smoothed her dress and decided to take the day as it came—one awkward toast and one lovingly prepared soufflé at a time.

On the other hand, Alexandra remained outwardly nonchalant about the brunch, the kind of casual disinterest she'd perfected over years of being dragged to her mum's endless events. Another social gathering, another chance to be politely bored—so what? Yet, beneath her composed exterior, a spark of curiosity lingered.

At least this time, she wouldn't be entirely on her own. Ruth was intriguing, though Alexandra couldn't quite figure out why. There was something about her—a quiet confidence, maybe, or the way she seemed to carry an air of mystery without trying. It was enough to make Alexandra wonder if this brunch might hold something unexpected after all.

Ruth, however, had no time for such musings. She and Conney had been planning how to get Alexandra to feel Ruth could be a close friend all morning. If they had known what Alexandra was thinking about Ruth, they would've been pleased with their progress, realising they were closer to success than they had imagined.

When Anna and Alexandra arrived, the warmth at the door was undeniable. Stanley beamed as he took in Anna's smile, and Ruth's heart lifted at the unexpected brightness in Alexandra's expression.

"Thank you for having us," Anna said, handing Stanley a plate of homemade cookies.

"You didn't have to go to the trouble," Stanley replied, but his smile betrayed how much the gesture meant to him.

"Oh, it's no trouble at all. Cooking relaxes me. And really, thank you for inviting us," Anna said, her sincerity shining through.

Stanley led them to the atrium, a sanctuary of lush greenery and vibrant blooms. It was his favourite place in the house—a haven he and his mother had cultivated together. For Ruth, it had always been a place of comfort, and now Stanley hoped it would be the perfect setting for this special meal.

To his surprise and delight, Alexandra lit up at the sight. "Oh, wow! Look at the *Monstera deliciosa*! I love how it looks like Swiss cheese. And the jasmine hanging over the table—it smells divine. You even have a Kentia Palm, it is so graceful. Oh, Mum, This feels like paradise!"

Anna chimed in, her voice warm with admiration. "It's absolutely stunning, Stanley. You've created something magical here."

Ruth was floored. If she had known Alexandra's love for plants, she could have used it as a conversation starter much earlier.

Stanley was proud that he had something that both Anna and Alexandra loved. The brunch unfolded in a way none of them had expected. Conversations about plants morphed into stories of travel and exploration, and Stanley felt a pang of regret for not having given Ruth the same kind of adventures. But for once, regrets were drowned out by the genuine joy of connection.

Ruth loved it. Both she and Stanley forgot about the mission as they wrapped themselves in the warmth of the conversation and enjoyed the occasion.

After the meal, Stanley and Anna's conversation unfolded in the garden, where the afternoon sun's warmth mirrored their dialogue's openness. They spoke of their daughters with unmistakable pride, exchanging stories of their quirks and ambitions.

Anna touched briefly on her divorce, framing it within the broader context of misaligned values. "It was never going to work," she admitted with a shrug. "But it taught me what I truly care about. That's why my mother and I are fighting my brother in court. The media empire was supposed to be split between us, but he took everything—and turned it into a propaganda machine for the government."

Stanley nodded, his empathy genuine. "That must be so difficult. But it's inspiring to hear how you've channelled it into advocacy. You're doing something that matters."

Meanwhile, Ruth and Alexandra found themselves laughing, dancing, and having unexpectedly deep conversations in Ruth's room. Alexandra confided in Ruth her worries about her boyfriend's drinking, and together, they navigated the complex emotions surrounding it. Ever the strategist, Ruth gently shifted the conversation toward Alexandra's family's media empire.

"Do you spend much time around your great-uncle's business?" Ruth asked casually, her tone light despite the weight of the question.

Alexandra hesitated for a moment as if testing the waters. "Why do you ask?"

Ruth's heart skipped, worried she might've pushed too soon. But she leaned into their shared camaraderie, her voice softening with vulnerability. "I've just always been fascinated by the media world. I want to be a journalist someday," she admitted, pausing to let a trace of hesitation creep into her voice. "But the way so many journalists seem... tethered to the government makes me uneasy."

Alexandra's guarded expression softened. "If you want to be an independent journalist, prepare to be disappointed," she said, a rueful smile playing on her lips. "Thomas and I talk about it all the time."

Ruth blinked, surprised. "I didn't realise you and Thomas were close."

Alexandra gave a slight shrug, her earlier hesitation giving way to honesty. "We try to keep it quiet. Both of our families—well, not my mother, obviously—but the rest? They're part of the problem. It's... complicated."

A flicker of panic crossed her face as she realised how much she'd said. "I shouldn't have told you that. Please, just forget it."

Ruth hesitated, choosing her words carefully. "I'm glad you told me," she said gently. "I feel the same way. I don't talk about it much, but I dream about doing something meaningful— something that makes the world more fair for everyone."

Alexandra's eyes lit up with recognition. "That's such a relief to hear. Have you talked to Thomas about this?"

"No," Ruth replied honestly. "His father's very connected, and... well, my dad recently lost a case to Mr. Caldwell. It was about the Albersteen Community."

Alexandra's jaw dropped. "That was your dad's case? I had no idea. My mother and I followed it closely. We were heartbroken when it didn't go through."

"This is something you and your mom care about?" Ruth asked, intrigued.

"Absolutely," Alexandra said firmly. "She and my grandmother are fighting to open up the media, to stop all these archaic policies from shaping our future. They're in court right now, battling my great-uncle. My grandmother was supposed to inherit one of the media businesses, but he consolidated everything into his control. It's outrageous—supported by the Crumpt government, no less. A complete betrayal of what my family was supposed to stand for."

Ruth's mind raced. She wanted to press further but knew it was better to tread carefully. Instead, she met Alexandra's frustration with empathy. "I can't imagine how frustrating that must be. You and your family are so brave to fight back."

By the time Anna and Alexandra prepared to leave, none of them wanted the day to end. There was an undeniable connection—an energy that left Stanley hopeful.

Ruth and Alexandra had made plans to include Alexandra in Ruth's study sessions with Thomas. The idea of expanding their circle excited Ruth, even though she did admit to herself she liked being on her own with Thomas. For now, though, the thought of diving deeper into the causes she cared about—alongside Alexandra—was enough.

As Alexandra left, her goodbye carried a spark of something new, something unspoken yet undeniable. Stanley watched from the doorway, a small smile on his face. Whatever this day had planted, he knew it had the potential to grow into something extraordinary.

Chapter 16
Uncovering Shadows

Thomas's expression clouded as Ruth mentioned Alexandra joining their study session at his place.

"Did I do something wrong?" she asked, her voice laced with concern.

"No," he said, his tone measured but uneasy. "Did she tell you that we're good friends?"

"She did," Ruth replied, her brow furrowing. "Why? Is that a problem?"

"Not exactly," Thomas admitted, his reluctance clear. "It's just... I like our sessions with just the two of us."

Ruth hesitated, caught off guard by the admission. Her cheeks warmed as she blurted out, "Me too."

For a moment, the air between them was thick with unspoken tension. Then, scrambling to soften the moment, Ruth added, "But I really like her, Thomas. I want to be friends. Should I cancel?"

Thomas hesitated, then gave her a small, reassuring smile. "No, it's fine," he said, his tone softening. "Really."

His reaction was puzzling but oddly comforting, leaving Ruth with a mix of optimism and curiosity about how this new dynamic might unfold. She felt this wasn't a step back but a step toward something better. Perhaps, with Alexandra in the mix, their conversations could delve even deeper into the things that mattered most.

And maybe, just maybe, she'd find a way to keep those moments she cherished with Thomas intact, too.

Later that day, Ruth found herself stepping into a world unlike anything she'd experienced. Thomas's chauffeur waited at the school steps, and as she and Thomas approached, she noticed him shift uncomfortably.

"Before we get there, I just want to say… this isn't how I would live if I had a choice," he said, his voice tinged with embarrassment.

"What do you mean? Is something wrong?" Ruth asked, tilting her head in concern.

"No, it's just… my dad likes to show off. The house—it's more of a statement than a home. I just didn't want you to hold it against me."

Ruth smiled, trying to ease his discomfort. "I'm sure it's fine, Thomas."

But as the car pulled up to the estate, Ruth realised he wasn't exaggerating.

The house was a monument to excess, perched on a hill as if to ensure its dominance over the landscape. The driveway, paved with imported marble, twisted and turned like an extravagant red carpet. A massive fountain at its centre featured gilded dolphins, their forms illuminated by LED lights. It was as if every inch of the property screamed, *Look how much we can afford.*

The façade was a cacophony of styles, from Roman columns to floor-to-ceiling glass windows, crowned with a doorway encrusted with gemstones. Inside, the overwhelming opulence continued. Marble floors glistened under the light of crystal chandeliers, and the rooms were filled with priceless art arranged more for effect than appreciation.

"It's… a lot," Ruth said tactfully as they passed an enormous dining room that seemed fit for royal banquets but, according to Thomas, was rarely used.

"I told you," Thomas said with a rueful smile, leading her through the maze of cold, overdecorated spaces. When they finally reached his wing, the atmosphere shifted entirely.

This space felt human. Warm wooden tones replaced marble, and the walls were lined with personal photos and bookshelves crammed with well-worn volumes. The couch looked inviting, its cushions soft and worn, a stark contrast to the sterile grandeur of the rest of the house.

"Now this feels like you," Ruth said with a smile, settling into the couch.

Thomas's face lit up. "I'm glad you think so."

Before either could say more, Alexandra's voice broke the moment. "Hey, you two! Are we going to study or just stare at each other all day?"

Startled, they both jumped and laughed, joining Alexandra to spread out their books.

The door opened about an hour into their session, and Alan Caldwell walked in. Ruth immediately noticed his sharp suit, perfectly tailored to exude power—a stark contrast to her father's more relaxed appearance.

"Thomas, a word," Alan said, his tone clipped.

Thomas looked tense as he rose and followed his father into the hallway. Though the door closed behind them, Alan's voice carried through.

"What are you doing bringing Rossiter's daughter here? You should've cleared this with me."

"I'm sorry, Dad. I didn't think it would be an issue," Thomas replied, his voice subdued.

"Well, it is. She is not to go anywhere outside your wing. Is that clear?" Alan snapped.

"Yes, Dad," Thomas said quietly.

When Thomas returned, he tried to mask his unease, but both Ruth and Alexandra could see through it.

"Are you okay?" they asked in unison.

"Yeah, I'm fine," Thomas said, forcing a casual tone. "Dad just wanted to make sure we didn't mess up the house. And, uh, he said we should stay in my wing."

Ruth frowned, finding the explanation odd. Alexandra was less subtle. "Your dad's such a dick," she said bluntly. "He's probably worried we'll uncover all the shady things he's up to."

To Ruth's surprise, Thomas didn't defend his father. He simply nodded a quiet confirmation that spoke volumes.

They returned to their studies, but Ruth couldn't shake the unease. Alan Caldwell's sharp tone and Thomas's subdued reaction gnawed at her thoughts. The encounter felt significant, though its meaning eluded her. As the chauffeur drove her home, Ruth stared out the window, a quiet determination forming. The Caldwells' world was a puzzle, and she had a sense she'd only begun to uncover its edges.

When Ruth arrived home, she barely had time to take off her coat before Stanley's voice called out from his study.

"How was studying at the Caldwells?" he yelled.

Ruth stepped into the room, closing the door behind her. "It was... strange," she said, her voice tinged with curiosity. "The house is a crazy maze of ridiculous richness."

Stanley chuckled softly. "I can imagine. Did they treat you well?"

"Yes, fine," Ruth replied, her tone hesitant. "But Mr. Caldwell wasn't comfortable with me being there."

Stanley's posture shifted, his interest sharpening. "You specifically, or any of Thomas's friends?"

"Me specifically," Ruth said firmly.

"Interesting," Stanley mused, rubbing his chin. "That means he definitely has something to hide. I didn't think he'd keep anything sensitive at home, though."

"What sort of things should I be looking for?" Ruth asked, her voice dropping to a whisper.

Stanley's gaze turned serious. "You, my dear, should be looking for *nothing*. Focus on your studies while you're there. If you hear anything as part of that, great, but under no circumstances are you to go searching for anything. It's far too dangerous."

Ruth nodded, but her mind raced. "Do you think Thomas is involved in his father's... misdeeds?" she asked.

"No," Ruth answered her own question before Stanley could. "He's scared of his father, but he's not like him. Both he and Alexandra called him a... well, a dick. Excuse the language, Father."

Stanley waved a hand dismissively. "Under the circumstances, you're excused. That's good to know about Thomas. But as I said, keep your focus on your studies. I still don't like the idea of you going there. Can't you study here instead?"

"Dad, it's more likely Thomas will open up while Alexandra and I are at his place," Ruth explained, her tone calm but insistent.

Stanley sighed, reluctant but resigned. "Fine. But we take it one session at a time. Agreed?"

"Agreed," Ruth said with a determined nod.

As she left the study, Ruth couldn't help but feel the weight of what Stanley hadn't said. Alan Caldwell's discomfort wasn't just about her presence—it was about what she might uncover. And while her father's warning rang in her ears, she couldn't help but wonder: how deep did the secrets go, and how close was she to finding out?

Chapter 17
Building Bridges, Weighing Risks

Ruth and Stanley's debrief with Raymond that week was brimming with energy and optimism. The room felt lighter than usual, and their conversation was filled with excitement about the connections they were building with Anna, Alexandra, and Thomas.

"I think we can trust Anna," Stanley said, his tone carrying the conviction of someone who had found a kindred spirit.

Raymond's expression shifted unexpectedly, and the lightness in the room dimmed slightly. The change caught Stanley off guard.

"Oh, Raymond," Stanley said quickly, his enthusiasm softening into concern. "I'm sorry if I'm getting ahead of myself. Maybe we need to pull back. I was just... excited. It feels like we've found someone who really shares our values."

Before Raymond could respond, Ruth jumped in. "I agree with Dad! Anna seems like she'd align so well with the Alliance. She could be a really valuable asset."

Stanley glanced at Raymond, his voice steady but earnest. "Have we overstepped? I know we're still relatively new to the Alliance, but I like to think I have a good instinct about people."

Raymond studied Stanley for a long moment, his silence weighty but not unkind. Finally, he spoke. "You two are doing incredible work, and it's clear how much you've invested. What you've done so far is invaluable. But," he paused, his tone deliberate, "there's a lot to consider here. I'll need to discuss this with leadership before we decide on the next steps."

He leaned forward slightly, his gaze unwavering. "Please don't take any risks. Stay the course you're on. Keep building those connections, but at no point expose yourselves—not until we've spoken again."

Stanley and Ruth nodded, the gravity of his words sinking in, but their determination remained intact.

After Raymond left, Stanley and Ruth wandered into the garden. The quiet hum of nature surrounded them as they walked in companionable silence, letting the conversation settle.

It was Ruth who eventually broke the stillness. "Do you think we've gone too far? Me going to the Caldwells? You suggesting we could trust Anna?"

Stanley sighed, his gaze resting on the horizon. "I don't know. But I trust Raymond. He wouldn't steer us wrong. So, for now, we keep doing what we've been doing and wait to hear back before we make any big moves."

Ruth nodded, a small smile forming. "Okay. It's been fun so far, though, hasn't it?"

Stanley glanced at her, unable to suppress a grin. "Yes. It has been fun."

She nudged him playfully. "There's a home game this weekend. Should we ask Anna if we can sit with her and Alexandra?"

Stanley chuckled. "Yes, let's do that. No matter what Raymond decides, it'll be good to keep building those connections."

And with that, their resolve felt lighter, their path forward more hopeful, as they strolled back toward the house together.

The game was another nail-biter, but fortunately, Haleberry won out in the end. Thomas had spent time giving Ruth a rundown of how the game was played. This new knowledge helped her enjoy the game more than previously. She now knew Thomas was a Quarterback. His role was critical. He needed to be focused, as it was his role to give commands to other players and start most plays.

Although Ruth hated the way he was constantly thrown to the ground, she wanted him and the team to do well. At one point, she found herself cheering because he got up from what seemed like a crushing blow, but everyone else didn't seem to notice.

Although Stanley had asked Anna and Alexandra out for dinner after the game, Anna had refused, saying she had another engagement. Although disappointed, he was grateful that he'd gotten to spend the time he did with her.

As Stanley and Ruth were leaving the stadium, he received a call. It was Raymond.

"Hey, Stanley," Raymond said, his tone warm but tinged with something... urgent. "If you and Ruth can swing by my place on your way home, there's something I'd like to show you. Oh, and if you haven't eaten, we'd love to have you both stay for dinner."

Stanley glanced at Ruth. "Ruth, Raymond's invited us to stop by. What do you think? Up for it?"

Ruth hesitated. No one had invited her back to the party after the game. Thomas had left with his dad, and Alexandra was going to a concert. She felt a flicker of relief—at least this evening wasn't over yet.

"Sure, why not?" she said with a slight shrug.

 Raymond's house was nestled at the edge of town, charming and unassuming. Inside, the warmth of the home enveloped them. The savoury aroma of the dinner Raymond had cooked wafted through the air, and Raymond's wife, Mary, entertained them with her characteristic humour and sparkle. Her stories were vivid, and Stanley found himself laughing more than he had in weeks. For Ruth, it was fascinating—Mary's anecdotes painted a picture of her mother she'd never heard before.

As dinner wrapped up, Raymond glanced at his watch. His expression sharpened.

"Alright," he said, his voice suddenly more serious. "There's something I want to show you. Follow me."

Stanley raised an eyebrow, and Ruth exchanged a curious look with him. Could this finally be the moment they'd been waiting for? They had speculated for weeks about the possibility of Raymond sharing something about the Alliance, but they could never have anticipated what was to come.

Raymond led them down a narrow staircase to the basement. When they reached the bottom, he pressed a hidden button on the wall. A trapdoor opened on the floor with a quiet click and a mechanical hum, revealing a second stairway leading deeper underground.

Stanley let out a low whistle. Ruth's eyes widened.

"After you," Raymond said with a grin, gesturing toward the stairs.

The air grew cooler as they descended, and the faint hum of machinery grew louder. At the bottom, a brightly lit room came into view, lined with sleek computer equipment humming with energy. And then—there she was.

Anna. Standing confidently by a bookcase that looked like it held more secrets than books.

"Hi, Stanley. Hi, Ruth," Anna said, her voice steady and calm.

Stanley and Ruth froze. Their gazes snapped to Raymond, their faces filled with shock and questions.

"I can explain," Anna said quickly, stepping forward. "I'm already part of the Alliance. Not Alexandra. She knows... well, enough to be cautious. But she doesn't know *this*. And it's vital that we keep it that way."

Stanley stood motionless, studying her. "Anna, you've always been vocal about your opinions. Doesn't being part of the Alliance put you at risk? You're not exactly discreet."

Anna smirked. "Exactly. That's my cover. My family and friends think I'm just an outspoken contrarian—a thorn in their side, sure, but harmless. My name shields me. No one would suspect me of this."

Raymond stepped in. "Stanley, Ruth, this is important. The Alliance operates under strict secrecy. Only the leadership knows every member's identity. It's rare—*extremely* rare— for us to reveal one member to another like this. But after much discussion, we agreed this was an exception worth making.

Raymond turned to Stanley, his tone low and deliberate. "Your friendship with Anna has been growing naturally. If people see you together, it won't raise suspicion. And with what's coming, the two of you need to trust each other completely."

Stanley's heart thundered in his chest. His gaze darted between Anna and Raymond, the weight of the moment bearing down on him like a physical force. This wasn't just a casual revelation—this was a seismic shift, one that he could feel rippling through everything he thought he knew.

Finally, he drew a steadying breath. "Alright," he said, his voice firm but tinged with unease. "You have my attention. What's next?"

Anna's lips curled into a knowing smile, a flicker of determination in her eyes. "Given how naturally people have seen our friendship grow, I think it's time to bring you to some events. Places where you can meet people of importance to the Alliance. Are you comfortable with that?"

Stanley's brow furrowed. He couldn't hold back the question that burned in his mind. "Is that why you befriended me? Did you know I was with the Alliance from the start?"

Anna's expression softened, but her gaze didn't waver. "Stanley, I had no idea at first. It's exactly as Raymond said—our friendship grew naturally. I only learned about your connection to the Alliance when Raymond approached me."

Stanley tried to keep his face neutral, but the wave of relief was impossible to ignore.

Anna turned to Ruth, her expression growing more serious. "Ruth, it's absolutely critical that you don't share any of this with Alexandra. She's not like you. She's grown up surrounded by these people—her friends, her family—and I want her to form her own opinions before I tell her about my connection to the Alliance. Please do not mention anything about the Alliance. Can you promise me that?"

Ruth nodded without hesitation, her voice steady. "Of course, Anna. I'll keep it to myself."

Anna exhaled, the tension in her shoulders easing. "Thank you, Ruth. That means more than you know."

The room settled into a heavy silence, the unspoken truths binding them all in a fragile but undeniable unity. For Stanley and Ruth, this was more than just a secret—it was the beginning of something far more significant than either of them had imagined.

Chapter 18
Keeping Secrets

Keeping the Alliance a secret had always felt like a heavy responsibility, but now, knowing Anna was a member and being unable to discuss it with Alexandra? That felt cruel. Ruth couldn't shake the guilt.

Conney, ever the voice of reason, tried to soothe her. "Ruth, it's for Alexandra's own good. Like Anna said, she needs to form her own opinions. Plus, if she knew, she could accidentally expose herself to her family and friends."

Ruth sighed, frustrated but resigned. "I get it, I do. But I can just *tell* she'd be all in if she knew about the Alliance."

"Well, that's not your call," Conney replied, her tone firm but not unkind. "Anna's a smart woman. If she's keeping this from Alexandra, it's not on a whim. She's thought it through."

"True," Ruth muttered, a rueful smile tugging at her lips. "But I'm allowed to feel guilty about it, right?"

"Of course! Feel all the guilt you want," Conney said with a smirk. "Just don't let it show, or you'll give the game away."

Later, Ruth, Thomas, and Alexandra travelled together to Thomas's house, their conversation bouncing with energy.

"Do you think Mrs. Porter will ever run out of bizarre drama assignments?" Thomas groaned. "Pretending to *be* a sewing machine? What even *was* that?"

Alexandra laughed. "Honestly, I thought it was pretty liberating. When else do you get to hum and vibrate like that without people calling you weird?"

"I was aiming for *industrial vintage chic,*" Ruth added with mock seriousness. "I think I nailed it."

The laughter spilled over as they pulled into Thomas's driveway. Remembering Thomas's recent photography project, Ruth turned to him with a genuine smile. "Thomas, those photos you submitted for the charity. They were incredible. You captured so much heart. Are you sure you shouldn't study art in college?"

Thomas's face clouded for a moment. "Thanks, Ruth, but it's not up to me. My father has already decided what I'm studying. Business. No debate."

Ruth frowned. "Why don't you tell him what you really want?"

Alexandra interjected gently, her voice tinged with understanding. "You don't know his dad, Ruth. Have a conversation about *feelings*? Let alone changing his mind? It's... not how it works in Thomas's house."

The mood dipped, and silence settled over them as they parked. But it wasn't a heavy silence—it was a companionable one, thick with unspoken solidarity. Once they were safely tucked into Thomas's wing of the house, their laughter and warmth began to bubble back, unbroken by the world waiting just beyond the walls.

Then Alexandra said thoughtfully, "Thomas," her voice low but charged with determination. "What if we found something to hold over your father? Something that could make him change his mind?"

Thomas's eyes widened, his concern immediate. "Whoa, slow down. You know my dad—if he even *suspects* someone's been snooping through his stuff, he'll lose it. Completely."

Alexandra leaned forward, her tone sharp but persuasive. "You know his schedule, right? Pick a time when he's away for a few days. What do you really have to lose? A miserable life dictated by your father—or a chance at one you define for yourself?"

Ruth stayed silent, her heart pounding. She couldn't deny she was rooting for Alexandra's bold idea, but the thought of getting involved felt risky.

Thomas turned to her, his gaze seeking reassurance. "What do *you* think, Ruth?"

Ruth hesitated, choosing her words carefully. "Thomas, I think it would be a disaster if you couldn't follow your passion. Not just for yourself but for the people who could benefit from your work. Your photos have so much heart—they deserve to be seen."

The room fell silent, the weight of the decision pressing down on all of them. Finally, Thomas broke the tension. "Alright. He's away for three days next week. Let's do it then."

When Ruth told Stanley, his disapproval was immediate.

"Ruth, that's a terrible idea," he said, his brow furrowed with worry.

Raymond, who had joined their briefing session, echoed his concern. "This sounds incredibly risky, Ruth."

Ruth's voice was steady, though her own nerves simmered beneath the surface. "It's not my idea, and Mr. Caldwell won't even be there. But I need to know—what exactly should I be looking for?"

The conversation spiralled into a back-and-forth of doubts and logistics, and neither side was entirely comfortable with the plan. Eventually, they decided to consult Anna.

Within the hour, Anna arrived, her expression tight with worry. Her first thought was for Alexandra.

"If they're determined to do this, they'll go through with it whether I'm there or not," Ruth said, her tone pragmatic.

"If Ruth goes along, at least she can be an extra set of eyes to keep them out of trouble," said Anna.

The discussion circled endlessly, but eventually, they all agreed. Ruth would go, both to keep Alexandra safe and to gather what information she could.

Anna and Raymond meticulously briefed Ruth on what information could make a difference. Two key targets emerged: documents tied to the communities Alan Caldwell seemed intent on acquiring and anything about mines. They suspected Caldwell was orchestrating the construction of tunnels to link these communities, creating a clandestine underground network—for reasons they didn't fully disclose.

The stakes were clear. This wasn't just about helping Thomas—it was a thread that could unravel something far more significant. As the plan took shape, Ruth felt its gravity settle heavily on her shoulders. It was a dangerous gamble, but the potential impact on both Thomas and the Alliance was undeniable.

In the days leading up to their mission, Ruth, Alexandra, and Thomas discussed every detail, their conversations alternating between bursts of nervous energy and uneasy silence. By the time the day arrived, their usual chatter had evaporated, replaced by a tense quiet on the ride to Thomas's house.

As they drove, Ruth suddenly had a thought she couldn't ignore. "Thomas," she began hesitantly, breaking the silence, "I just realised I've never met your mother. Does she live with you?"

Thomas and Alexandra exchanged a quick glance, a fleeting look that carried years of unspoken understanding. Thomas finally answered, his voice subdued. "No. She left when I was really young. I don't even remember her. And my dad doesn't keep any photos of her."

Ruth's heart ached at the sadness in his tone. "I'm so sorry," she said softly. "I shouldn't have asked. I didn't mean to pry."

Thomas managed a small, bittersweet smile. "It's okay. Really. I'm used to it."

The car fell silent again, but the air between them felt heavier now—weighted by Thomas's quiet sorrow and Ruth's remorse for stirring it. Yet beneath the tension, there was an unspoken understanding: they were in this together, ready to face whatever the mission would bring.

Chapter 19
Shadows Beneath the Surface

The trio spent the first half hour in nervous chatter, their words light but their movements betraying the tension thrumming beneath the surface. The air in Thomas's wing felt stifling, the weight of what they were about to do pressing on them. Finally, summoning their courage, they rose and headed to his father's study.

The door loomed before them, solid and unyielding, but Thomas approached it with an unsettling calm. He keyed in the code he knew by heart. The lock gave a sharp beep, and the door clicked open. They slipped inside, their footsteps muffled as they moved with purpose, hyper-aware of the risk of discovery.

The study felt like an extension of Alan Caldwell himself: grand, intimidating, and meticulously ordered. A massive desk commanded the room, its sheer size dwarfing Ruth's expectations. Floor-to-ceiling bookshelves lined the walls, the faint scent of polished wood and leather giving the space an air of wealth and dominance. It was a place meant to inspire awe—and fear.

They paused for a moment, each of them scanning the room as if daring the shadows to reveal something incriminating.

"We need to split up," Thomas said quietly, his voice taut. "Alexandra, check the bookshelf. Ruth, go through the desk. I'll work on cracking the computer."

They nodded, the plan simple yet fraught with uncertainty. Ruth approached the desk, her heart hammering in her chest. The drawers slid open with a faint groan as she rifled through documents, her fingers trembling as she scanned each page. Alexandra moved methodically along the shelves, her eyes darting over the titles. Meanwhile, Thomas crouched before the computer; his brow furrowed in concentration as he worked on bypassing the password.

It wasn't until Ruth glanced toward the lounge area that she noticed it—a model tucked into the corner. She approached it cautiously, drawn by the intricate details. It was a replica of a multi-story factory, complete with eerily lifelike human figures. But it was the bottom floor that stopped her cold. At first glance, it looked like a design schematic, but as she leaned in, she realised it was a labyrinth of tunnels, winding and branching like some twisted mind map.

"Thomas," she called softly, snapping a few pictures with her phone. "You need to see this."

He glanced up briefly but shook his head. "It's weird, but I don't think it's anything useful. Keep searching."

Ruth bit her lip, frustrated, but turned back to the desk. Just as she opened another drawer, Alexandra gasped sharply. The sound cut through the room like a knife.

"What is it?" Ruth hissed, spinning toward her.

Alexandra's face was pale. "I pulled a book—the Old Testament—and the whole wall moved!"

The three of them froze as the bookshelf slid aside with a low mechanical hum, revealing a dimly lit corridor. Light flickered along its walls, casting long shadows into the study.

"Do we go in?" Alexandra whispered, her voice trembling.

Thomas squared his shoulders. "We didn't come this far to back out now."

They descended a steep, narrow staircase, the air growing colder with each step. At the bottom, they emerged into a cavernous room. Alexandra and Ruth halted, their breaths catching in their throats.

"There are people down here," Alexandra whispered, backing up.

"Wait," Thomas said firmly, stepping forward. "They're not people. They're robots."

The girls turned to him, disbelief written across their faces. Ruth's eyes darted back to the rows of figures standing motionless in the dim light. As she looked closer, her stomach twisted. They were lifelike—uncannily so. Each had unique features: different skin tones, hairstyles, and facial expressions as if designed to mimic individuality.

"How do you know?" Ruth asked, her voice barely audible.

Thomas pointed to a female figure near the front. "I've seen her before. She was in my father's office once. He said she was a prototype."

Ruth stepped closer, her curiosity overriding her unease. She reached out and brushed her fingers against the figure's skin. The sensation made her recoil. "It feels real," she whispered, her voice thick with disbelief.

Thomas nodded grimly. "There's a factory somewhere making these, but I don't know why he has so many here—or what he plans to do with them."

They moved cautiously through the rows, counting at least thirty robots—male and female, each the same height but eerily unique in their details. The room was oppressive, the silence broken only by their hushed breathing, and the sound of Ruth's camera.

"This is... wrong," Alexandra murmured. "What could he possibly need them for?"

Thomas shook his head. "Whatever it is, it's not good."

The weight of the discovery pressed down on them as they retraced their steps, their minds racing with unanswered questions. Back in the study, Alexandra slid the Bible back into place, sealing the hidden passage.

"Okay, back to work," Thomas said, though his voice lacked conviction.

Ruth's gaze fell on a small trophy on Alan's desk. Turning it over absently, she noticed an engraving on the base. "Thomas, do you think this might be the code for his computer?" she asked.

Thomas took it, studying the numbers and letters. "Only one way to find out."

He entered the sequence, and the screen flickered to life. A voice interface greeted them: "Good morning, Alan. What do you need?"

The three exchanged uneasy looks before Thomas quickly switched to a keypad mode. He typed his father's name into the search bar, and a list of files populated the screen. Their eyes darted over the titles until Ruth pointed to one.

"'Alan Caldwell – Parole Schedule,'" she read aloud. "What's that?"

Thomas opened it, and the document filled the screen. It was a release record from the Florida Penitentiary, dated 2031. Alan Caldwell had served five years for fraud.

Ruth stared at the screen, stunned. "Thomas... did you know?"

"No," Thomas muttered, his jaw tight. "He's always putting people down, acting like he's untouchable. I never would have guessed."

They printed the file and carefully restored everything before retreating to Thomas's wing. The tension of the night finally broke as they collapsed into the chairs, their breaths coming fast.

"Thomas, what are you going to do?" Ruth asked.

"I don't know," he said, bitterness creeping into his voice. "But he's a hypocrite."

"Maybe that's why he's so critical," Alexandra offered gently.

Thomas scoffed. "It doesn't excuse him. He acts like perfection itself, and look at this."

For now, they agreed to keep the discovery quiet. But Ruth couldn't shake the feeling that their night's work was just the beginning—and that Alan Caldwell's secrets were more profound than they imagined.

Chapter 20
Secrets, Schemes, and Human Machines

Ruth had pulled it off—she'd snooped through Alan Caldwell's office, uncovered a trove of secrets, and walked away without raising suspicion. The fact that she'd managed to deceive her friends left a sour taste in her mouth, but she was also pretty proud of herself. Not everyone could break into a billionaire's lair and live to tell the tale, let alone return with evidence.

When Ruth got home from Thomas's place, the house was quiet. It wasn't until she reached Stanley's office that the muted buzz of voices tipped her off. Peeking through the half-open door, she saw Anna and Raymond deep in conversation with her father, Stanley, their heads close together like they were plotting the heist of the century.

Ruth pushed the door open, and they all shot upright like kids caught raiding the cookie jar. Stanley was the first to recover, crossing the room in a few strides to envelop her in a hug.

"It's okay, Dad. I'm fine," Ruth said, patting his back awkwardly.

Stanley pulled away but kept his hands on her shoulders. "I know, I know. There's just... so much happening, and when I'm not with you, I can't help but worry."

Raymond cleared his throat, cutting through the moment. "Come sit down," he said, gesturing to the lounge.

Stanley shut the door and ushered them all to the lounge. He sat close to Ruth while Anna and Raymond took seats across from them. Their expressions were a mix of curiosity and anticipation.

"How did it go?" Anna asked, leaning forward. "Is Alexandra okay? Did she suspect anything?"

"Alexandra's fine, and we're in the clear," Ruth said. "Actually, she made the biggest discovery. There was a hidden basement full of..." She paused for effect. "Human robots."

Raymond blinked. "What do you mean, *human robots?*"

Ruth pulled out her phone, swiping to the photos she'd taken. "See for yourself."

Anna took the phone first, her eyes narrowing as she examined the images. "There were rumours, but... this? They look *real*. How real were they in person?"

"Uncannily real," Ruth said. "I touched one— it felt like human skin. Warm, even."

"Jesus," Raymond muttered under his breath.

"What do you think it means?" Ruth asked, glancing between them.

"We're not sure yet," Raymond admitted. "But we do know Caldwell's continuing to try buying up entire communities and pushing for specific crops to be planted. Whatever he's planning, there's complexity to it."

Ruth hesitated. "There was more. I saw a model of what looked like a factory—it wasn't labelled, but it seemed... ominous. On the lower floor, there appeared to be tunnels"

Raymond leaned forward, narrowing his eyes as Ruth swiped to the photos of the factory model. "This could be his plan for the Cyprus mine land," he murmured, his voice heavy with scepticism. "But what the hell is he planning to *do* with it?"

"And one more thing," Ruth said, her tone sharpening. "We found a file on his computer.

It was from the Florida Penitentiary—he was jailed for fraud and released in 2031."

Anna's jaw dropped. "Thomas didn't know about this, did he?"

Ruth shook her head. "No, and he was *pissed*. He printed a copy of the file, saying it might be the one thing he can use against his dad."

Stanley let out a low whistle, the sound more venomous than surprised. "I *knew* that man was rotten. A snake through and through. Always has been, always will be."

Everyone turned to him, startled by the venom in his voice. Stanley straightened, muttering, "Sorry. It's just... I've always known he was evil. There's no way a man like that ever truly reforms."

"Well," Anna said, still examining the model photos, "it's obvious he's getting outside funding. No way he could bankroll all this on his own."

"Exactly," Stanley agreed. "And he's not exactly hiding his wealth. And the way he bought up Albersteen? That wasn't just flexing wealth. It was *strategy*."

Raymond nodded, his expression grim. "We suspected he had powerful backers, and this all but confirms it."

As the weight of their conversation settled over the room, Stanley leaned back against the couch, his mind racing. The puzzle pieces were coming together, but the picture they formed was more unsettling than he could have imagined.

The next morning at school, Ruth spotted Thomas surrounded by his usual entourage of boisterous friends. But when he saw her, he broke away from the group, triggering a wave of wolf whistles and jeers.

"Aw, Thomas! Taking pity on the new girl already?" one of them shouted.

"She's not even in your league!" another added, their laughter echoing down the hallway.

Ruth rolled her eyes, unimpressed. She knew their taunts were rooted in their own insecurities, and besides, she was confident in her budding friendship with Thomas. Whatever they thought, she wasn't about to let it get to her.

As he approached, Ruth gave him a small smile. "How are you holding up? Yesterday must've been a lot."

Thomas sighed, running a hand through his hair. "Yeah, it was. I always suspected my dad had skeletons in his closet, but now I've got proof. It's... weirdly satisfying."

Before Ruth could reply, Alexandra appeared behind her like a gust of wind. "Hey, you two! Feeling less traumatised today

"Seems like we're good," Ruth said with a grin. "What about you?"

"Oh, I'm fine, but my mom went full *helicopter parent* when I told her. She's all, 'Be careful, Alexandra! Don't mention it to anyone!' Ugh." She threw her hands up in mock exasperation.

"You told your *mom*?" Ruth asked.

"Of course," Alexandra said with a shrug. "Don't worry—she's super trustworthy."

"She really is," Thomas added. "Anna's helped me out a ton, and she can definitely keep a secret."

Ruth let out a relieved breath. If Alexandra's mom was the one who leaked anything, Ruth could keep her own role under wraps. Testing the waters, she added, "I told my dad, too."

Thomas raised an eyebrow. "Do you think he'll say anything?"

"No," Ruth said quickly. "But he might be able to help us down the line. He's good at digging up dirt—if you ever want him to look into your dad's past, just say the word."

Thomas hesitated, then nodded. "I'll think about it."

With that, they headed to class, unsure of what lay ahead but united in their shared unease.

Ruth and Alexandra sat at their usual table at lunch while Thomas stayed with his crowd. The separation didn't bother Ruth; they had their own rhythms, and besides, she had her own plans brewing.

By the end of the day, the trio had agreed to meet at Ruth's house on Saturday morning. With no school events or games to distract them, it was the perfect time to regroup.

It was a Conney day—finally. After school, they met at their usual spot. Ruth had been counting down the days to this moment. Conney had been on holiday with her mother, and so much had happened in her absence that Ruth barely knew where to start.

It took an entire hour to get Conney up to speed. Ruth spared no detail, and Conney, ever her sharp and curious self, hung on every word. By the time Ruth finished, Conney looked positively electrified.

"You're incredible," Conney said, leaning forward with her hands clasped. "You've managed to keep your cover *and* dig up all this dirt? Ruth, I'm in awe."

"Thanks," Ruth said with a modest shrug, though her cheeks tinged pink. "But honestly, it's not like I'm some kind of master spy. Most of it just... fell into my lap."

"Don't downplay it," Conney shot back, shaking her head. "Falling into your lap or not, you had to say the right things and make the right moves. That takes skill, Ruth."

Ruth sighed, stirring her drink absentmindedly. "Maybe. But I'm starting to feel... conflicted. I really like Thomas and Alexandra. They might think I've just been using them if they ever find out about my ulterior motives."

Conney reached across the table and placed a reassuring hand on Ruth's. "Listen, you're doing this for a good reason. If it ever comes to light, you'll explain it. And they'll understand if they're as good as you say they are."

Ruth gave a small, uncertain smile. "I hope so. I really do."

Conney leaned back in her chair, her tone lightening. "Besides, if they do find out, we'll cross that bridge when we get to it. Until then, you keep doing what you're doing—because you're killing it."

Ruth chuckled, some of the tension easing from her shoulders. Conney always had a way of putting things into perspective, even when everything felt impossibly tangled.

Chapter 21
A Night of Warmth, a Morning of Battles

Stanley and Anna had officially fallen into a rhythm of "date" nights—though neither had called it that out loud. These evenings began predictably, dissecting their daughters' latest escapades. Ruth and Alexandra's proximity to Alan Caldwell, the local villain incarnate, was enough to leave any parent twitchy. They swapped worries like war stories and shared advice they had carefully curated with input from Raymond.

But tonight, Stanley had a plan—a bold, nerve-wracking, heart-pounding plan. He was done orbiting the "just friends" zone like some lovesick satellite. It was now or never. The internal debate had gone on long enough, aided by the voice of his late wife, Janey, in his head. He knew he was projecting, but her imagined words had become his compass.

"Stanley, stop overthinking. You're still the man who won me over, and you'll win her too. But seriously— move it along, or she'll think you're just her therapist."

Thanks, Janey. No pressure.

When he picked Anna up, he went for broke. "I was wondering if we could park everything tonight—no kids, no Caldwell—just focus on us. You and me."

Anna's expression softened, her lips curling into a gentle smile. "I'd like that."

Score one for Stanley.

The restaurant, one of Anna's favourites, seemed to conspire in his favour. The candlelight flickered just so, the wine flowed smoothly, and even the food seemed extra sumptuous. Laughter bubbled between them as naturally as the clinking glasses, and Stanley felt like more than a widowed father for the first time in ages.

By the time they returned to Anna's doorstep, he'd mentally rehearsed his next move about a hundred times. His palms were clammy, his pulse racing.

"May I kiss you?" he asked, his voice barely above a whisper.

Anna's grin turned mischievous. "I thought you'd never make a move." And before he could second-guess, she closed the gap, her lips pressing against his in a kiss that was warm, lingering, and electric.

Their arms wrapped around each other, the kiss deepening with the kind of passion that knocked the breath out of Stanley.

"Why don't you come in tonight?" Anna murmured against his lips, her voice playful yet inviting. "Alexandra's at a friend's, and I've already done my housework."

He laughed, the tension melting away as they stumbled through her front door, unable to let go of each other.

Once they reached her bedroom, Stanley hesitated briefly, fumbling not out of reluctance but sheer nerves. It had been so long, and the vulnerability was almost overwhelming. But Anna was patient, her touch steady, her smile reassuring. She made him feel like a man rediscovering himself, and the night unfolded in equal measure with tenderness and fiery intensity.

When Stanley woke, sunlight was filtering through the blinds, and Anna's hair tickled his nose as she rested her head on his chest. He didn't want to move—didn't want to break the spell of her warmth against him—but responsibilities loomed.

His voice was soft, almost regretful. "Anna, are you awake?"

"Mmm," she murmured, half-asleep.

"I'd love to stay in bed with you all day—believe me, I would—but I've got meetings. I need to go home and change before anyone notices."

Anna cracked one eye open, her smile lazy and content. "Thank you for last night. I hope it was as lovely for you as it was for me."

Stanley chuckled, brushing a kiss against her hair. "Lovely is an understatement. It was one of the best nights of my life. Thank you, Anna."

She tilted her head to kiss his neck, then rolled away so he could get up. A pang of loneliness hit him as the cool air replaced her warmth. He had already missed her closeness, even as he dressed.

As Stanley slipped out the door, the grin on his face refused to fade. For the first time in years, he felt alive in a way that wasn't tied to duty or loss. Whatever came next, he thought, he could face it.

But "whatever came next" hit like a freight train.

Stanley's first meeting of the day was with Major Jones, the beleaguered mayor of yet another community under siege by Alan Caldwell, Captuna. As they sat across from each other, the weight of the conversation pressed down on Stanley like an iron yoke.

"I lost the Albersteen case," Stanley said, his voice heavy with honesty. "Maybe another lawyer would be better for your cause."

"We know," Major Jones replied, his tone resolute but tinged with desperation. "But no one else will take the case. You have the experience, Stanley. You understand what's at stake. And most importantly—we trust you."

The words hit Stanley square in the chest. Trust was a precious commodity, and hearing it so earnestly was both humbling and daunting. He took a breath, his mind already racing with the challenges ahead.

"Okay," he said finally. "I'll take the case. But I need you to understand—this will be an uphill battle. The government is on Caldwell's side. Even if we manage to manoeuvre around the policies that lost us, Albersteen, they could just draft new ones to stop us."

"We understand," Major Jones said, his voice steady but grave. "We don't have a choice."

As Major Jones left, the room felt quieter and heavier. Stanley leaned back in his chair, staring at the ceiling as if it held the answers. The stakes were towering, and he knew all too well the storm that lay ahead. Caldwell wasn't just a man; he was a machine fueled by wealth, influence, and a disregard for morality.

If there was a way to beat him, Stanley needed to dig deeper—much deeper. His mind circled back to Caldwell's past, particularly his conviction for fraud. Few people knew about it, and Stanley was beginning to wonder if that skeleton in Caldwell's closet could be used to bar him from legally buying up entire communities. It was a long shot, but it was something.

"I need to call Raymond," Stanley muttered, grabbing his phone.

Raymond's voice crackled on the other end, calm but edged with tension. When Stanley explained the situation, Raymond let out a low whistle.

"Taking the case gives us a legitimate reason to investigate Caldwell," Raymond said, his tone thoughtful. "That's good. But you know as well as I do—this guy doesn't play fair. And this is another distraction from the Alliance's bigger goal. If we keep chasing him, the larger mission to destabilise the government will lose momentum."

Stanley pinched the bridge of his nose. "I know. But this is more than a legal case, Ray. It's a chance to expose him. It could ripple out if we can show the public who he really is. People are already scared of him—this could turn fear into action."

Raymond sighed. "You're not wrong. But this fight's going to be long, Stanley. Brutally long. We need to be ready for that. No shortcuts, no quick wins. If Caldwell's proven anything, it's that he's relentless. We need to be more so."

Stanley nodded, though the weight of Raymond's words sat like a stone in his stomach. They were right to fight, but the fight was far from fair—and even farther from over.

As he hung up, Stanley stared out the window. The sun was bright, mocking the shadows stretching across his thoughts. For all the passion and fire he felt last night, today was a stark reminder of the battles ahead.

This wasn't just about winning a case or taking down Caldwell. It was about enduring—about outlasting a man who seemed unstoppable and proving that trust, grit, and truth could still matter in a world that felt increasingly hostile to all three.

With a deep breath, Stanley stood. The road ahead was steep, but he'd walked hard paths before. He only hoped he had enough fight left to see it through.

Chapter 22
An Unexpected Adventure

Alexandra couldn't make the Saturday session after all, and Thomas had been called away on an urgent photography assignment he couldn't refuse. There had been a fire in the storeroom on the University Campus, and they needed photos. Not one to let an opportunity slip by, he asked Ruth, "Want to come along?".

Ruth hesitated for only a moment before saying yes. When Thomas arrived on his motorbike to pick her up, she did a double-take. She had expected a car, or maybe his driver, but a motorbike? That was new.

Handing her a helmet, Thomas grinned. "First time on a bike?"

Ruth laughed nervously. "Let's just say I'm glad Stanley isn't here to see this. He'd probably have a heart attack."

As she climbed on, the thrill of the moment hit her—wind in her face, the hum of the engine beneath her. It felt like a tiny rebellion, a slice of freedom.

When they arrived at the site of the fire, the acrid smell of smoke hit them before they saw the charred remains of the campus storeroom. The scene was a mess of blackened walls and heaps of ash, a stark reminder of what fire could do.

"Is this how you usually approach assignments?" Ruth asked as they surveyed the scene.

"You mean solo or on my bike?" Thomas replied with a smirk.

"Both, I guess."

Thomas nodded. "I prefer working alone sometimes. It gives me space to think. No one breathing down my neck."

"Do you want me to wait outside? I don't want to cramp your style," Ruth teased.

Thomas turned to her with a smile that was both earnest and unguarded. "Not at all. You're different, Ruth. I like having you around."

Ruth felt her cheeks warm but decided to play it cool. "Do you think you could show me how you work?"

"Absolutely. Let's go."

The damage inside was worse than it had appeared from the outside. It was clear someone had deliberately piled papers and set them ablaze. The walls were streaked with soot, and the air still held a lingering, smoky heaviness.

Thomas, ever the professional, moved with calm precision. He showed Ruth how to use his camera and explained how lighting and angles could transform a simple shot into something extraordinary. Ruth soaked it all in, delighted by Thomas's patience and encouragement.

They lost track of time as they worked side by side—taking photos, studying the scene, and sharing easy conversation. They laughed over silly jokes and swapped stories, their connection deepening with each passing moment.

Eventually, Thomas declared they had everything they needed. "How about lunch? There's a café not far from your place."

Ruth agreed, her excitement bubbling over. For the first time in a long while, she felt utterly free—free to be herself, to explore, to talk about things that genuinely interested her.

Over sandwiches and coffee, they shared more about their passions. Ruth talked about her love for painting, especially capturing the flowers in her family's atrium. Thomas opened up about his dream of joining a choir and how much he loved playing the piano, though his father disapproved.

The day had been perfect—until Ruth and Thomas pulled up at her house.

Stanley was perched on the front step like a hawk, his face an unsettling blend of relief and simmering worry. Ruth felt her stomach drop as she climbed off Thomas's motorbike, tugging off her helmet with an awkward smile.

"Ruth," Stanley began, his voice carrying both fatherly authority and genuine concern, "I've been trying to reach you all afternoon. Your comms were down, and I was worried sick. And a *motorbike*? Really? I'd have appreciated a heads-up before my daughter reenacted a scene from *Fast & Furious*."

Ruth cringed. "I'm so sorry, Dad. I didn't think about it. Thomas invited me to tag along for a photography assignment, and we ended up grabbing lunch. It was completely safe."

Thomas stepped forward, every bit the respectful gentleman. "Mr Rossiter, I apologise. I should've asked for your permission beforehand. The assignment was on short notice, and I didn't mean to cause any concern."

Stanley studied Thomas for a moment, then exhaled heavily, his posture softening. "Just... let me know next time. Both of you."

Ruth nodded fervently. "Promise!"

Thomas gave a polite nod, his earnest demeanour enough to earn a tiny glimmer of reluctant admiration in Stanley's eyes— though he masked it quickly.

As Thomas drove off, Ruth bounced past her father, practically floating up the steps and into the house.

Stanley followed, closing the door with a determined thud. "Are you serious about Thomas?" he asked, his tone hovering somewhere between casual inquiry and full-blown interrogation.

Ruth stopped mid-stride, a mischievous smile tugging at her lips. "What do you mean?"

"You know exactly what I mean," Stanley replied, narrowing his eyes. "Is he your *boyfriend*?"

Ruth's cheeks turned pink. "Boyfriend? No! Well... maybe? I don't know. How do you tell?"

Stanley rubbed the back of his neck, clearly regretting this line of questioning. "Usually, one of you would ask the other if you'd like to start dating. That's... sort of how it works."

"Dating?" Ruth let out a burst of laughter, the kind that comes from genuine surprise.

"Yes, *dating*," Stanley said, his voice tinged with both exasperation and awkwardness. "I wasn't prepared for this conversation, but I think it's time we had it."

"Had what? The talk about *dating*?" Ruth giggled again, clearly enjoying her father's discomfort.

"Yes," Stanley said firmly, though a nervous edge crept into his tone. "There are things you need to know."

Ruth waved him off with a dramatic flourish. "Tell me later. I'm going to my room." Her voice was light, almost sing-song, as she skipped toward the stairs.

Stanley watched her go, a storm of emotions brewing. He hadn't expected *this*. It hadn't even crossed his mind that *The Talk*—the capital *T* kind of talk—was now firmly on his to-do list. He paced for a moment, weighing his options, before muttering to himself, "I need Anna. She'll know what to say."

Later that evening, his face etched with a mix of worry and confusion, he asked Anna, "Isn't Ruth too young for a boyfriend?

Anna smiled gently. "She's fourteen, Stanley. That's normal. Have you talked to her about… you know, sex?"

Stanley's cheeks turned red. "Sex? No! She's my baby. It hadn't even occurred to me."

Anna sighed, equal parts amused and exasperated. "Well, that's going to have to change."

"I have no idea what to say," Stanley admitted, his tone bordering on panic.

"If you like," Anna offered, "I can talk to your mother first, see if she's already had the conversation with Ruth. Maybe she's ahead of us."

Stanley shook his head emphatically. "My mother? Talk about sex? Oh, no. I can guarantee she's never mentioned it to Ruth. And there's no way she'd be open to discussing it with either of us."

"Okay," Anna said, suppressing a laugh. "Then I'm happy to step in. Though honestly, Ruth might already know more than we think."

Stanley frowned. "I'm not so sure. She's been pretty sheltered. But I'd appreciate it if you'd try. I think she'd be more comfortable hearing it from you than me."

"Alright, I'll handle it," Anna reassured him.

Stanley hesitated, his concern deepening. "I'm worried about Thomas being the boy."

Anna placed a calming hand on his arm. "I get it. His father's reputation is… troubling. But Thomas is a good kid. And, Stanley, you can't choose for her. If you push too hard, you'll only push her away. You'll have to trust her judgment, and she's a smart girl."

Stanley let out a long sigh, nodding reluctantly. "You're right. I just hope she knows what she's doing." Anna smiled, her voice warm with reassurance. "She's growing up, Stanley. And as much as it scares you, she's going to be okay."

Chapter 23
The Breaking Point

Ruth's life was transforming in ways she had never imagined, and she embraced it with boundless enthusiasm. She began regularly accompanying Thomas on his photography assignments, her curiosity growing with every click of the camera. Her fascination turned into passion, and by the time her fifteenth birthday approached, she boldly asked Stanley for her own camera.

The middle of 2067 marked the start of an unforgettable chapter that would profoundly shape Ruth in beautiful and bittersweet ways.

The year began with joy and discovery. Ruth had cemented a meaningful friendship with Alexandra, a bond she treasured deeply. Her time with Conney brought laughter and comfort, and to her surprise, Alicia and Arabella began inviting her to parties. While she suspected their invitations had more to do with Thomas being her boyfriend than her own merits, she didn't mind. These social events gave her the access she needed for her larger mission—a purpose she kept close to her heart. But to her surprise, she found herself genuinely enjoying the camaraderie and new experiences.

Stanley, always the protective yet supportive father, had laid down one firm rule: Ruth and Thomas were to spend most of their time together at his house. He promised not to intrude but insisted they stay under his roof when possible. Ruth didn't mind; they weren't home often between school, Thomas's photography assignments, and their shared love for concerts.

On the rare occasions they visited Thomas's house, Ruth found herself curious but careful. She respected Stanley's wishes, understanding that his rules came from a place of love and trust. Thomas, ever considerate, didn't push boundaries, and their relationship thrived in its unique rhythm.

Ruth was thriving too. She poured her energy into her growing love for photography, finding new ways to express herself and see the world. Her days were filled with vibrant connections, artistic exploration, and an optimistic drive that carried her forward.

But life has a way of intertwining light and shadow. While 2067 and 2068 was a period of growth and newfound joys, the following year would bring challenges Ruth never anticipated—ones that would test her spirit and alter her forever. Yet, even in moments of uncertainty, she would rise, carrying with her the resilience and optimism that had always defined her.

It was one of those rare afternoons when Ruth found herself at Thomas's house. They were studying, hands intertwined across his desk, a quiet moment of peace and connection. That serenity shattered the instant Alan Caldwell, Thomas's father, walked in, his presence like a storm brewing on the horizon.

"Thomas, I need to speak to you," Alan demanded, his voice sharp and cold.

Thomas stood immediately, his demeanour calm but tense. He followed his father into the hallway, leaving Ruth frozen, her hand now empty and trembling.

"What is *she* doing here? I told you I didn't want you seeing her!" Alan's voice roared, echoing through the walls.

"Dad, please, keep your voice down," Thomas pleaded his tone firm but edged with desperation.

That was the moment Ruth realised the truth. They hadn't avoided Thomas's house because of Stanley's rules—it was because Alan didn't approve of their relationship. Today, Thomas had taken the risk because he believed his father would be out of town. Her chest tightened as the pieces fell into place: Thomas's brief, dismissive comments about his father, the tension he carried, the way he deflected questions about his home life.

Stanley had warned her not to involve herself in anything risky while he was dealing with the Captuna case. Yet here she was, not because of espionage, but because of her relationship with Thomas—a connection that now seemed more fragile and fraught than she'd realised.

"Don't you tell me to keep my voice down!" Alan bellowed. "This is *my* house, and I'll speak however I damn well please."

"Dad, I don't care what you say," Thomas retorted, his voice shaking with anger and defiance. "I like her, and we're going to keep seeing each other."

A deafening bang startled Ruth. She bolted to the door, peeking out just in time to see Alan dragging Thomas by his hair toward the study. Ruth's heart raced, fear gripping her chest like a vice.

Alan paused, turning his steely glare toward her while still clutching Thomas. "You, get your things and wait at the front door. Someone will drive you home."

Ruth's eyes darted to Thomas, whose face was pale with fear. "Dad, please don't do this. Don't do this, Dad, please," he begged, his voice cracking.

But Alan was relentless, dragging Thomas away as though his pleas meant nothing.

Tears streaming down her face, Ruth shouted, "Please don't hurt him, Mr Caldwell! I'll leave right now and never come back, but *please* don't hurt him!"

Alan didn't respond. Ruth, trembling, gathered her belongings and ran to the front entrance as fast as her legs would carry her. The chauffeur was already waiting, his expression unreadable. She climbed into the car, sobbing uncontrollably.

Before the car had fully stopped in front of her house, Ruth jumped out and burst through the door. "Dad! Dad! Dad, where are you?" she screamed, her voice cracking with urgency.

Stanley appeared from the atrium with Anna, both alarmed by her panicked cries.

"Ruth, what happened?" Stanley asked, his tone steady but filled with concern.

Practically inconsolable, Ruth managed to choke out the details between sobs. The moment Stanley understood what had happened, he stood tall, his face set with fury. "I'm going over there," he declared, heading toward the door.

Anna grabbed his arm firmly. "No, Stanley, you can't. It'll only escalate things."

"I have to do *something*. That poor boy," Stanley shot back, his voice breaking with anger and sorrow.

"I'll go," Anna said resolutely. "I've known Alan a long time. It makes sense for me to handle this."

"It's too dangerous, Anna," Stanley argued, his protective instincts flaring.

"Not for me. Alan would never harm me, and you know it. This is the best way," Anna replied, calm but unyielding.

"Please, Anna," Ruth begged, her voice trembling with desperation. "Please help Thomas. It's all my fault. If I hadn't been there—"

Anna knelt and embraced Ruth tightly. "It's not your fault, Ruth. Not at all. I'll go right now."

Stanley pulled Anna into a brief but firm hug. "Keep your comms on. Call me the moment you're out of there."

"I will," Anna promised.

Without another word, she left, her resolve unwavering. Ruth stood with Stanley, clutching his arm, her heart heavy with fear for Thomas. She prayed silently that Anna would return with good news.

It felt like an eternity before she did, her expression weary and solemn. She had been at Alan's house for two tense hours, and the weight of the visit hung heavy in the air as she delivered her report.

Her voice was calm but tinged with sadness as she began. "He knew immediately why I was there. I didn't even need to say anything. He led me to his study, where Thomas was sitting in a chair. He looked shaken but unharmed."

"Thank goodness," Ruth whispered, her hands trembling as she clung to Stanley's arm. Stanley exhaled audibly, relief washing over him—not just for Thomas's safety, but for Anna's as well.

"Alan sent Thomas to his room," Anna continued. "But before he left, Thomas was adamant about one thing: he wanted to make sure you were okay, Ruth. He asked me to tell you that he's fine and that he's sorry for everything." Anna's eyes softened as she met Ruth's tearful gaze.

Ruth nodded, her lip quivering. "I was so worried about him," she murmured.

Anna sighed deeply as if the weight of her words were heavier than she anticipated. "Alan and I went back and forth for quite some time. He was insistent that his rules were his rules, and that Thomas had to abide by them, no exceptions. He was defensive, even angry, but eventually, I got through to him."

Her gaze shifted to Stanley. "I reminded him that discipline doesn't mean breaking a child's spirit and that whatever his frustrations, there are lines that should never be crossed. By the time I left, Alan had calmed down. I don't think he'll harm Thomas physically, but…" She hesitated, her voice faltering.

"But what?" Stanley pressed gently, and his brows furrowed with concern.

Anna glanced at Ruth, then back to Stanley. "Alan's still angry. His control over Thomas is rigid, and it's clear this isn't the first time tension like this has flared. I don't think it's something that will resolve easily. Thomas is caught in a storm that's been brewing for years."

Ruth's face crumpled, and tears spilled down her cheeks. "It's all my fault. If I hadn't been there—"

Anna quickly stepped forward, placing a firm yet gentle hand on Ruth's shoulder. "No, Ruth. This isn't your fault. Thomas's relationship with his father is complicated, and he sees you as a representation of your father, and this legal battle is getting nasty. If anything, being with you gives Thomas strength."

Stanley nodded solemnly. "Anna's right. This isn't on you, Ruth. But we'll need to tread carefully. Alan's temper and his stubbornness could make things worse if we're not mindful, and this case isn't helping"

Anna straightened, her resolve clear even in her exhaustion. "I'll check in with Thomas when I can, and I'll keep the lines of communication open with Alan—whatever it takes to make sure Thomas stays safe. But we have to be prepared."

Ruth and Stanley exchanged a worried glance, but Anna's steady presence gave them a glimmer of hope.

Chapter 24
Hope Beyond the Storm

Thomas was absent from school, his comms eerily silent. Every attempt Ruth made to reach him ended in failure. She knew there was only one place he might be—his house. But the thought of facing Alan Caldwell again, of risking his unpredictable anger, made her stomach churn. She couldn't go there, not after everything that had happened.

The uncertainty gnawed at her all day, and her worry was a constant weight. Then, as she turned the corner toward her locker, she froze. Ms. Ellis was standing in front of Thomas's locker, carefully packing its contents into a box.

"Why are you doing that?" Ruth asked, her voice thin and trembling.

Ms. Ellis looked up, her expression neutral. "Thomas is transferring schools. I believe he's going to study in Europe. Isn't that a wonderful opportunity?" she said brightly, as if delivering good news.

Ruth's world seemed to tilt on its axis. Her knees buckled, and she collapsed onto the floor as she processed the weight of what she'd heard.

"Ruth!" Ms. Ellis cried out, rushing toward her.

She wasn't unconscious, but she couldn't move. Numbness spread through her body, and her thoughts spiralled into chaos. Because of her, Thomas's life was being turned upside down. Because of her, Alan had sent him away. The reality of it crushed her, and tears began to stream uncontrollably down her face. She barely registered Ms Ellis calling for another teacher. Together, they helped her to the sick room, where the school nurse dabbed at her face and asked gentle questions. But Ruth couldn't respond. The words were too heavy, the pain too raw.

Time blurred. She didn't know how long she lay there, staring blankly at the ceiling, when she felt strong arms scoop her up—familiar, comforting arms.

"Oh, honey," Stanley's voice was soft yet filled with desperation. "Please, please be okay."

Ruth mumbled, her voice cracking under the weight of her grief, "Dad… he sent him away."

"I know, sweetheart. I know," Stanley replied, his voice low and steady, but his grip on her tightened as though he could shield her from the hurt.

Ms. Ellis stood nearby, her expression etched with regret. "Stanley, I'm so sorry. I didn't realise… I never thought she would react like this. I should have been more considerate."

Stanley shook his head, a gentle but weary smile on his face. "It's not your fault. There's been a lot going on, and I think this was just… the final straw for her. Please, don't worry. I'll take her home now."

He turned to Ruth, crouching slightly to meet her gaze. "Can you stand, sweetheart? Can you walk with me to the car?"

Ruth nodded faintly, her legs shaky but functional. Stanley helped her to her feet, and as they stepped into the hallway, Alexandra was waiting, her face a mask of worry.

"Are you okay?" Alexandra asked, stepping closer.

Ruth forced a small, fragile smile. "I'll be fine. I just… I just need some time."

Stanley had already called Raymond, who arranged for Conney to be waiting at their house. The moment they stepped through the front door, Conney rushed forward, pulling Ruth into a warm, grounding hug.

"Dad, I'm okay now," Ruth whispered, leaning into Conney's embrace. She glanced up at her friend. "Conney, I'm so glad you're here."

With that, Ruth and Conney walked arm-in-arm to her room, their steps slow but steady. Stanley remained in the foyer, watching them disappear down the hallway. He let out a deep sigh, his shoulders slumping.

He wasn't sure what to do next, but one thing was certain: Ruth needed him now more than ever, and he would do whatever it took to help her through this storm.

Conney, always the steady voice of reason, gently placed a comforting hand on Ruth's shoulder. "At least you know he's safe," she said softly, her words meant to anchor Ruth in the storm of her emotions.

Ruth shook her head, her voice breaking as tears welled up again. "That doesn't help, Conney. What if I never see him again?" Her heart ached with the thought. Thomas had become such a significant part of her life. How could she go back to school knowing he wouldn't be there?

Even if she somehow adjusted, she knew she wouldn't escape his presence entirely. His name would echo through the halls for months to come—whispered by classmates, mentioned in passing by teachers, tied to the high-profile story of his sudden departure. Ruth buried her face in her hands. "I don't know how to do this without him," she admitted, her voice barely a whisper.

Conney wrapped an arm around her, pulling her close. "You're stronger than you think, Ruth. I know it feels impossible now, but you'll find your way through this. And who knows? Life has a funny way of bringing people back together when you least expect it."

Then, like a spark in the dark, Conney's voice ignited a flicker of hope. "We still have a job to do, Ruth. If we can bring down Alan Caldwell, we might also free Thomas. Let's focus on that."

Ruth's eyes widened, the weight of despair lifting ever so slightly. A renewed sense of purpose began to take root in her chest.

"You're right, Conney. We *can* do something. We can fight back and help Thomas."

Conney smiled, her tone warm yet steady. "That's the spirit. We'll figure it out together, step by step. But for now, let's take a breather. Tonight, we'll cuddle up, watch a movie, and recharge. Tomorrow, we'll start fresh and make a plan."

Ruth nodded, a small but genuine smile breaking through her tears. "Thank you, Conney. I don't know what I'd do without you."

"That's what best friends are for," Conney replied, guiding Ruth toward her bed. As they settled in, the glow of the screen casting soft light in the room, Ruth felt a flicker of hope steadying her heart. She wasn't alone in this, and together, they would fight for a better tomorrow.

The next morning, Stanley was pleasantly surprised by Ruth's energy. The decision to have Conney stay over had clearly been the right one. Her usual spark had returned, and she seemed more determined than ever. However, if Stanley had known what the two girls were quietly planning, his relief would have quickly turned into concern.

Chapter 25
Shadows of Power

Anna and Raymond arrived at Stanley's office mid-morning, their pace quickening as they sensed the weight of his urgency. Stanley's mind was racing—Caldwell's actions were growing more alarming, and the decision to send Thomas away gnawed at him. What if it accelerated whatever plans were already in motion? The unease tightened in his chest, and it was made worse by the message waiting for him that morning: a direct instruction to call President Crumpt as soon as he arrived. But Stanley had deliberately held off. He needed to speak to Anna and Raymond first. He had a sinking feeling this was about the Captuna Community case.

So far, despite the challenges, Stanley believed the case was moving in the right direction. He had carefully built his arguments around the damaging precedent set by Caldwell's victory in the Albersteen Community case, highlighting its profound impact on human rights. Momentum was on their side, and with each step forward, he felt more confident in their fight. And if push came to shove, he still had a decisive advantage—Alan Caldwell's criminal record, a revelation that could turn the tide once and for all.

On the surface, Anna and Raymond's visit appeared routine. They had recently founded an environmental charity, and Stanley was their legal advisor. This was the perfect cover—no one would suspect their meetings had a deeper, more pressing agenda.

Raymond and Anna positioned themselves carefully, ensuring they remained out of sight when Stanley made the video call. The moment he was put through, Stanley straightened in his chair and steadied his voice.

"Hello, Mr. President. I believe you sent me a message to call you. My apologies for the delay—I had pressing matters to attend to this morning."

"I understand," Crumpt replied. "I believe your daughter had an incident at school yesterday. How is she?"

Stanley's heart skipped a beat. How did he know about that? He masked his discomfort, responding evenly, "Oh, thank you for your concern. How did you hear about it?"

"There's very little I'm not aware of, Stanley." The President's tone was casual, but the weight of his words sent a chill through

Stanley's spine. It wasn't just an observation—it was a warning.

Drawing on years of experience as a lawyer, Stanley kept his expression neutral. "Of course. Well, she's okay now. We had some things going on at home that I think overwhelmed her, but she was fine this morning."

"Excellent." Crumpt's tone shifted. "The reason I called is that you need to hear this firsthand so you can advise the Captuna Community. The case is over. It's in everyone's best interest that they drop it."

Stanley stiffened. "I'm sorry, I don't understand. The case is running in their favour. Is there something I don't know?"

"Yes," Crumpt said flatly. "As a matter of public interest, the crops grown in that community must be protected as an essential resource for water purification. Today, we're passing a Bill that will designate the land as government property. We will then outsource the management of the community."

Stanley's pulse pounded in his ears. "Who will you be outsourcing the management to?"

"That isn't your concern," Crumpt said dismissively. "What you need to do is inform the community leaders that each resident will receive compensation and a guarantee that their homes and jobs will not be impacted."

Stanley clenched his jaw. "With all due respect, Mr. President, I can't see them agreeing to this. This is their land. Their lives."

"That's not your concern either, Stanley," Crumpt said, his voice turning cold. "The bill is being passed today. The land is too valuable to be left in the hands of civilians. This is just a courtesy call."

Stanley tried to push back. "But—"

"Stanley," Crumpt interrupted. "The community will be well compensated. I'll inform the judge personally. The case will be dismissed. Consider this a courtesy call. Goodbye, Stanley."

The call ended abruptly.

Silence filled the room. Stanley, Raymond, and Anna sat motionless, the weight of what had just happened pressing down on them like a crushing force. The shock was staggering. The fight the community had poured everything into had been wiped away with a single decision, their progress erased in an instant.

Stanley finally spoke, his voice hollow. "I don't know what I can do. The way he spoke… it's a done deal."

"There has to be a way," Anna said desperately.

Raymond exhaled, leaning forward. "We always knew this would be a long game. There were bound to be setbacks. We don't have the numbers to push back right now, but that doesn't mean we stop. It means we build. We strengthen the Alliance."

Anna's eyes burned with determination. "Then we stay underground. We get out into the communities and find those who will fight with us."

Stanley nodded slowly, the fire in his gut reigniting. "I need to speak to the Captuna Mayor."

Raymond leaned in. "Stanley, when you speak with him, feel him out. After he calms down, see if he's open to a long-term strategy. He might be willing to align with others who want to fight back if he is. Don't mention the Alliance yet. Just gauge where he stands."

Stanley straightened his shoulders. "Certainly, I would hate for him to have no hope. I'll see you both out, then call the Judge, then the Major."

The battle might've been lost, but the war was just beginning.

Naturally, Mayor Jones was furious. He refused to accept what Stanley was saying. "Stanley, we need to do something about this."

"I agree, but no matter what we do, it is unlikely to change anything in the short term," Stanley admitted. "I've spoken to the judge, and he said his hands are tied. He has seen the Bill and has no reason to believe it won't pass. As a result, we have a session before him tomorrow at 10:00 a.m."

"We'll all be there," said Mayor Jones.

"I appreciate that, and I'll do my best to argue the point, but I cannot see how we will win," Stanley said grimly.

"We will not give up," Mayor Jones declared.

"I understand, but being successful in the courts seems very unlikely. So, if you are interested, I can put you in touch with people who share your concerns. They are developing a strategy that may, in the long term, help us fight back," Stanley offered.

"Who are they?" Jones asked, his eyes narrowing.

"I can't tell you just yet. I will let them know if you want to learn more, and someone will contact you. Their identities must remain protected to ensure this fight continues without interference."

Jones hesitated, then gave a firm nod. "Well, Stanley, if tomorrow's outcome is as you say, then I will want to meet this person."

Unfortunately, it went precisely as Stanley had predicted. The community representatives were passionate, raising their voices in protest. Stanley fought hard, challenging the decision at every turn, but it was useless. The predetermined outcome stood, and the case was dismissed.

But the fire in their fight had not been extinguished. It was only just beginning.

Chapter 26
Into the Lion's Den

Ruth and Conney were determined to expose Alan Caldwell. No matter the risk, no matter the consequences. They knew if they breathed a word of their plan to Stanley or Raymond, it would be shut down immediately. The men were too cautious, too strategic. But this wasn't a time for patience—it was a time for action. So, they stayed silent, determined to do what needed to be done.

Thomas had vanished without a trace—no calls, no messages, and that terrified Ruth. He would have if he could have contacted her, which meant only one thing—he was being held somewhere and could not reach out. Every day that passed tightened the knot in her stomach.

On the surface, Ruth's conversations with Alexandra were just teenage chatter—venting about Alan, reminiscing about Thomas, hating the silence he'd left behind. But Ruth never told Alexandra what she and Conney were planning. It was safer that way—the fewer people who knew, the better.

The goal was simple: find Thomas, expose Alan, and uncover the truth behind the government's takeover of Captuna. The Alliance knew it was all connected—Alan's stranglehold on the Albersteen community and the government's sudden interest in the Captuna community—and that it reeked of corruption. But knowing wasn't enough. They needed proof. If they found it, they could help the Alliance bring both Caldwell and the government to their knees and free Thomas.

If Stanley or Raymond found out, they'd stop it before it even began. They saw dangers Ruth and Conney couldn't know, things the girls didn't, but Ruth and Conney were seventeen, fearless, and convinced they could handle it. They believed they were helping the cause but had no idea how much danger they were walking into.

The first step? A cover story. A harmless night out. They told their parents they were going to the movies, but in reality, they were headed straight to Caldwell's estate. Their target: Carl, Thomas's driver. He had been more than just an employee—he was Thomas's confidant. If anyone knew where Thomas was or what Alan Caldwell was planning, it was him.

Carl's apartment was tucked away on the far side of the Caldwell estate, with a separate entrance from the main house. The night air was thick with tension as Ruth and Conney stood at his door. Ruth knocked—once, twice—then waited.

A long pause.

Then, at last, the door creaked open just a fraction. Carl's sharp, wary eyes flickered between them. His face was shadowed, his body tense.

"What the hell are you doing here?" he hissed.

Ruth stepped forward, her voice urgent. "It's Thomas. We need to know where he is. Is he safe?"

Carl's expression darkened. He glanced over his shoulder, scanning the dimly lit hallway before exhaling sharply and stepping aside. "Get in. Quickly. Before someone sees you."

Inside, the room smelled of stale coffee and stress. Carl shut the door behind them and turned, his gaze locking onto Conney.

"Who's this?" he demanded.

"She's with me," Ruth said quickly. "She's helping. You can trust her."

Carl hesitated, his jaw tightening before he let out a heavy sigh. "You won't find him," he admitted. "I don't know where he is either. And that scares the hell out of me."

Ruth's stomach knotted. "But you were his driver. You must have seen something."

Carl shook his head. "I wasn't the one who took him. They sent someone else. One morning, he was just… gone. No warning. No goodbye. Alan told everyone he'd left to study in Paris, but we both know that's a damn lie." He ran a hand through his hair, his voice thick with frustration. "And there's nothing I can do about it."

Ruth clenched her fists. "Well, we're doing something."

Carl studied her for a long moment as if weighing whether to push them out the door or take a risk that could cost him everything. "What exactly are you planning?"

Ruth didn't blink. "We need Alan Caldwell's schedule for the next two weeks."

Carl exhaled sharply, rubbing his temples. "You realise if he even suspects I helped you, I'm dead? Not just fired. Dead."

"We wouldn't have come to you if we had another option," Conney said, stepping forward. "Please."

Another long silence. Then, finally, Carl nodded. "Fine. But listen to me—you have no idea what you're walking into. Alan is dangerous. If he catches you—" He cut himself off, shaking his head. "Just be careful."

Ruth's voice was steady. "We will. And Carl… I'm sorry if we're putting you in danger."

Carl's mouth twisted into something between a smirk and a grimace. "Don't worry about me. I have plans if things go sideways."

Minutes later, Ruth and Conney walked away clutching a piece of paper that could change everything—Alan Caldwell's schedule. Three days next week, he'd be out of town. That gave them a window.

And the second night he was gone, they'd make their move.

The break-in, it had to be flawless.

They told their parents it was another movie night. Conney was "sleeping over" at Ruth's. In reality, they were dressed in black, slipping through the shadows of the city. A taxi dropped them off a hundred meters from the back of the Caldwell estate.

The night was silent, except for the pounding of their hearts.

The back gate loomed ahead, a steel barrier standing between them and the truth. Ruth reached out, her fingers trembling slightly as she punched in Thomas's code. There was a pause.

Then—click.

The gate slid open.

They slipped inside, moving fast but keeping low. The estate stretched before them, its vast gardens dotted with lights. They ducked and weaved through the landscape, their eyes darting in every direction. There was no movement, no guards.

At the edge of the pool, the glass sliding door waited. Another hurdle. Another risk. Ruth swallowed hard, gripped the handle, and pushed.

Unlocked.

A trickle of unease ran down her spine. This was too easy.

They slipped inside, the cool air of the house wrapping around them like an omen. Alan's office was just ahead, down the hall. They moved quickly, their steps silent against the polished floor.

Inside the office, Ruth rushed to the computer. One deep breath. She typed in the password.

Access granted.

Her pulse raced. He hadn't changed a thing since Thomas left.

They worked fast, typing keywords: community names, government officials, contracts, and secret projects. Documents flooded the screen. They copied everything onto a flash drive, hands shaking.

An hour passed.

Then, the basement.

They pushed through the hidden door behind the bookcase and descended. The cold air hit them like a warning.

Rows of lifelike robots stood in eerie silence, their vacant eyes watching nothing—yet somehow seeing everything. There were more of them than before. The hairs on Ruth's arms stood on end as she snapped photos.

And then—

A sound.

A presence.

A shadow at the bottom of the staircase.

Alan Caldwell.

He stood there calmly, hands in his pockets, his eyes glinting with something unreadable.

"How stupid do you think I am?" His voice was smooth but laced with quiet menace. "Did you really think I wouldn't have security cameras all over this place? I was alerted the second you opened the gate."

Ruth's blood turned to ice.

Alan took a slow step forward. "What exactly do you think you're doing? And who the hell is this?" His gaze flicked to Conney.

"She's my friend," Ruth said quickly, trying to steady her voice. "We're looking for Thomas."

Alan let out a sharp, humourless laugh. "Thomas is in Paris. You already know that."

"He would have told me if he was leaving," Ruth shot back.

Alan smirked, his expression twisting with something cruel. "Why would he? You're just another girl to him."

Ruth refused to flinch. "I know you're lying. Let me talk to him."

Alan's smirk faded. "Don't be ridiculous. You'd only be a distraction."

Ruth fought to keep her voice even. He didn't know what they had—he didn't know about the flash drive in her pocket or the photos on her phone. She needed to keep this about Thomas.

Alan studied them for a long moment. His face was unreadable. Then, suddenly, his expression darkened.

"Upstairs. Now." Alan's voice was sharp, cutting through the tense silence like a blade.

He shoved them toward the couch, his grip firm, unyielding.

"Stand still," he ordered. His hands moved swiftly, patting them down. Then—his fingers closed around something in Ruth's pocket.

The flash drive.

Alan yanked it out and held it up, his expression darkening. "What is this?" His voice was a low growl, but the fury beneath it was palpable.

Ruth met his gaze, her heart pounding. There was no point in lying. "Files from your computer," she admitted. "We thought they might help us find Thomas."

A beat of silence. Then Alan exhaled a slow, quiet laugh—one that sent chills down Ruth's spine.

"You broke into my home," he murmured, almost amused. "Stole from my computer. Stuck your noses where they don't belong."

His smile stretched, eerie and deliberate.

"You think I'm just going to let you walk away?"

Then, he turned. Walked toward his desk. Pressed something.

A drawer slid open.

Ruth's breath caught in her throat.

He pulled out a gun.

Her world tilted.

Alan turned back to them, holding the weapon loosely in his grip. He tilted his head. "Do you know what this is?"

It crashed into them all at once—**this was real.**

Their game was over.

"Kneel." His voice was quiet. Dangerous.

Ruth's body was shaking. "Please, Mr. Caldwell—we won't tell anyone. We just want Thomas."

"Kneel." This time, it was a command.

Slowly, they obeyed.

Alan stepped forward, looming over them. The gun was cool against the back of Conney's head. "Now, little lady," he murmured. "Your friend Ruth here has gotten you into a mess you might not get out of. How do you feel about that?"

"Scared," Conney whispered.

Alan turned the gun on Ruth. "If I hear one word about what you've seen in my house—if you ever step foot on my property again—I will use this. Not just on you. But on your families. Do you understand?"

Ruth's breath came in shallow gasps. "Yes."

"Yes," Conney echoed, her voice barely a whisper.

Alan tucked the gun away. "Get up."

Moments later, Carl was summoned.

"Take these girls home," Alan ordered. Then, his voice dropped to something chilling. "And Carl—if I ever see them again, or you talking to them, there will be hell to pay."

The ride back was silent.

When Ruth and Conney finally stepped into Ruth's room, they collapsed onto the bed—shaking, breathless, terrified.

Then the tears came.

Chapter 27
And So It Began

Ruth and Conney stayed up all night, their minds racing, hearts heavy. The weight of their actions pressed down on them like a leaden cloud, and as dawn broke, they knew there was no choice but to come clean. The truth was too big, too dangerous to keep hidden any longer. They had to tell Raymond and Stanley—there was no other way.

Ruth's heart pounded as they made their way downstairs to Stanley's study. She knew he'd be getting ready for work, but the urgency in their steps made it feel like everything else had come to a halt. As soon as Stanley saw them, he knew something was wrong. The girls were different—eyes swollen, faces drawn, like they'd been carrying a burden too heavy for them to bear alone.

"Dad, we need to talk," Ruth's voice trembled slightly.

Stanley's concern was immediate. "Are you both okay? What's happened?"

Ruth hesitated, trying to find the right words. "Well… we're okay now, but last night… we did something we shouldn't have, and there might be consequences."

Stanley's expression tightened. "What?"

"We broke into Alan Caldwell's house," Ruth said, her words tumbling out. "And he caught us."

A chill passed over Stanley's face. "Oh my God. Did he hurt you?"

"No," Conney said quickly, "but he pulled out a gun."

"Jesus Christ, why didn't you come to me sooner? Why didn't you call out to me when you got home?" Stanley's voice was laced with panic.

"We thought we were doing the right thing," Ruth explained. "We were worried about Thomas."

Stanley let out a deep sigh, the tension in his shoulders softening just slightly. "The important thing is that you're both safe. Now go have some breakfast. I'll contact Raymond. I'm cancelling my appointments for the day, and you're both staying home from school. Conney, I'll call your mother, too." His concern was overwhelming but also grounding—like a steady hand reaching out in a storm.

Raymond arrived just as they were finishing breakfast. The air was thick with the tension of the unknown, and as they gathered in Stanley's study, it was clear the girls were still shaken, their nerves raw from the night before.

"What the hell were you thinking?" Raymond's voice was sharp, filled with disbelief.

"We had to," Ruth said, her voice strong despite the fear. "We knew you wouldn't let us, so we decided to do it ourselves—get into Caldwell's study, find something that could lead us to Thomas, maybe even uncover something useful for the Alliance."

Raymond's eyes turned to Conney, disappointment settling in his gaze. "Conney, I thought better of you. How could you let this happen?"

"I'm sorry," Conney said quietly, her head hanging low. "We thought he'd be out of town, that we wouldn't get caught."

Ruth stepped in, her voice firm. "It was my idea. I talked her into it."

"That's not an excuse," Raymond snapped. "Conney may be young, but she's a trained professional. She's a key player in the Alliance. What were you thinking, putting yourselves at risk like that?"

"I know, Uncle. It was rash. I'm really sorry," Conney's voice trembled, but she met Raymond's gaze. "But he doesn't know who I am or that we're with the Alliance. He saw me as just some silly friend of Ruth's."

Stanley's brow furrowed. "How could you know that?"

"He never asked my name," Conney said, her voice steadier now. "He saw Ruth as a lovesick teenager and thought I was just along for the ride."

"Are you sure he didn't make the connection?" Raymond pressed, still wary.

The girls explained everything—how Caldwell had pulled a gun, how they'd been terrified, and how, somehow, they had come out of it unscathed. When Stanley heard the whole story, his face drained of colour. He jumped to his feet, a mix of horror and disbelief. Ruth could see the weight of it all crashing down on him. Raymond, too, buried his face in his hands, unable to process the magnitude of what had just unfolded.

Stanley, shaking with relief, pulled the girls into a tight hug. "I'm so sorry," his voice cracked. "I never should have let you get involved in any of this, Ruth."

Ruth hugged him back, her own voice steady. "Dad, you didn't drag me into this. I *want* to be part of it. I want to make a difference. We can't let people like Alan Caldwell get away with this stuff."

"But you're too young and naive," Stanley said, his worry thick in his voice.

"I know, but I need to learn. I want to lead the Alliance someday and to do that, I need to experience things, even when they're hard."

She turned to Conney, her hand resting on her friend's arm. "And I want to be a better partner to you. I don't want to let you down like I did last night."

Conney smiled, squeezing her hand. "We're in this together, Ruth. Always."

Stanley paused, unsure of how to respond. After a long breath, he spoke with new resolve. "If we're going to keep doing this, we need to be better prepared. We both do."

Raymond, who had been quiet until then, nodded in agreement. "Stanley's right. The government keeps introducing new laws that weaken the power of the common people. And we keep losing battles—like the Albersteen Community case or the Captuna Community's fight. The Alliance has so much work ahead of it."

Stanley's eyes met Ruth's. "And your generation is going to be directly impacted. If we don't grow the Alliance and prepare for what's ahead, we'll lose our chance to make real change."

Raymond's expression softened, but his voice was firm. "We need to start building a better training program. And honestly, Stanley and Ruth, you two would be ideal candidates to help shape it. You're already involved, and you're learning quickly. It's time to take it to the next level."

Stanley nodded slowly, the pieces starting to fall into place. "You're right. It's time we stopped reacting and started preparing for what's ahead."

And just like that, Ruth's journey to the top of the Alliance began. Not with perfect steps, but with the courage to learn from mistakes, to face challenges head-on, and to keep pushing forward in the face of uncertainty. With every obstacle and every setback, she grew stronger—closer to her goal of making a real difference. She wasn't just learning to lead; she was learning how to change the world, one bold decision at a time. And no matter how tough it got, Ruth knew she was on the right path.

The legacy continues

https://books.by/woventale

www.ingramcontent.com/pod-product-compliance
Lightning Source LLC
Chambersburg PA
CBHW070502120726
47910CB00003B/1092